Finding Tane
Foggy Basin Season Two

Jamie Sands

Grey Kelpie Studio

Contents

Author Note

I've used New Zealand English for the spellings throughout this book, to reflect Tane's culture and my own. I could have switched between US English for Dillon and NZ English for Tane, but I thought that would be too confusing.

Thank you for understanding, Aroha nui, Jamie

This book is dedicated to the lovely BL Maxwell

Chapter One

Tane

L eaving L.A. was exactly what I needed.

I drove my rental car fast and blew the cobwebs out. I blasted music (K-Pop, a musical world away from the stuff I performed), rolled the windows down and relished the feeling of escape.

I'd done it. I'd made a stupid, rash decision and driven away from my life.

I'd left a message for my agent so he wouldn't send out search parties, turned off my phone and stuffed it in the bottom of my bag. I bought a new one and downloaded my favourite music app and that was all I needed. Booked a rental car and drove out of Los Angeles.

I pulled into Foggy Basin around three thirty in the afternoon, having taken a few stops for snacks and bathroom breaks, along with a visit to a roadside attraction for the hell of it. Hey, it wasn't everyday you got to see the world's biggest ball of string. Except I think there are at least five of the world's biggest balls of string around the country.

Anyway, I pulled into the cute little town and felt a wave of relief flood my brain, my blood pressure went down I was sure of it.

This little town was distinctly American, I saw flags here and there, and the signs and stuff felt like classic Americana. A movie from the 1950s just barely updated. The town was arranged down a single street, called Main Street, naturally.

I drove past my motel, determined to find some food and orient myself to the town before checking in and crashing for the night. I'd have a long shower and wash the memory of L.A. smog off my skin.

Main Street had a bookstore which also appeared to be a coffee shop, and there were a collection of other, cute little businesses. I looked forward to checking them all out in my own time. But first, the grocery store.

I found a parking lot and pulled in. I reached for a baseball cap out of habit and paused.

The folks walking up and down Main Street looked painfully normal. A grey-haired older lady walked down the road with a newspaper tucked under one arm. There were a couple of kids on scooters zipping down the sidewalk. A young man carried a bunch of roses, he looked nervous.

If I put on a baseball cap and my dark glasses, I was going to stand out like a sore thumb. I sat back in my seat and marvelled at the thought I'd actually be less conspicuous with my face bare. I shrugged, pocketed my phone and wallet and hopped out of the car. My legs protested at the stretch.

I headed up the street with a bona fide spring in my step. I was taking control of my life, I was anonymous in a cute little small town and my body felt like it might float away with the joy of it.

I had no idea what tomorrow held, and that was the most soothing thought I'd had in a while.

Foggy Basin Grocery had an automatic door, which I was slightly disappointed by. I'd hoped to have a little bell that rang, announcing my presence.

Inside the rows of shelves had an old-fashioned look to them, but otherwise it looked like any other mini-mart or large convenience store I'd been in. I thought of Four Square shops back home.

My stomach rumbled and I picked up a basket and started around the aisles.

I lost myself in the simple act of considering what food I wanted, letting my mind slide to focus on only this task, relaxing into it.

I didn't see anyone near me until I was reaching for a box of cereal on the top shelf when a hand reached past mine and retrieved the cereal for me. I startled, heart thudding, as I turned to the man who stood a good few inches taller than me.

"Here you are," he gave me a wide, even-toothed smile. His eyes were a warm sort of blue and his hair was trim, a mousey brown or ash blond color.

If my heart hadn't been thudding from the surprise it may have started from how cute this guy was. "Thanks?" I managed to say, voice lilting up at the end of the word — a hangover from my Kiwi accent that I was never able to fully erase.

"You're welcome, let me know if you need help reaching anything else, okay?"

The guy was wearing a smart, pressed, blue apron and the name *Dillon* was embroidered over the chest. The logo for the grocery was emblazoned on the pocket. "Thanks Dillon, you work here?"

I took the cereal and busied myself putting it in the basket, trying to pull myself together. I wasn't even that short, but he was tall enough to make me feel small and vulnerable, which I wasn't sure I liked.

"I own the place, as of fairly recently," Dillon said. "You're not from around here, are you?"

I swallowed and looked back at him — suddenly afraid this was about the color of my skin (Māori blood sometimes read as Mexican or even Middle Eastern to those who weren't familiar, and sometimes people were racist).

"Oh I just mean, your accent, I don't think I've heard it before." Dillon took a half-step back, as if he'd read my mind. He smiled again, a little more uncertain.

Relieved to have misread him, I shook my head. "Yeah, nah I'm from Aotearoa, uh. New Zealand?"

Dillon's eyes widened. "Oh wow. I don't know if we've ever had a New Zealander in Foggy Basin before."

I chuckled. "Well, I hope I don't disappoint you."

"I've always wanted to visit there," Dillon said. "After seeing Lord of the Rings, you know."

I did know. This was the number one thing that people overseas seemed to know about Aotearoa. Well, that and our nation's rugby prowess.

"Sure, everyone wants to be a hobbit," I said.

Dillon chuckled. "Are you staying long in Foggy Basin?"

I shrugged. "I dunno, a week or so at least." I had no real idea what my future held, after all.

"Well, I'm Dillon, like you saw on my apron." He held out a hand and I juggled my basket to shake it. He had a firm, sure handshake. I tried to match his energy.

"Tane." I pronounced it clearly so he wouldn't get it wrong.

"Welcome to town Tane," he started to back off. "Let me know if you need help finding anything."

"I will, thanks." I added another sugary cereal to my basket, some packets of instant ramen, a couple of snack cakes and bars of chocolate and a bag of chocolate chip cookies. For drinks I got instant coffee and some sports drinks. It wasn't exactly a healthy spread, but it was what my body wanted.

Some guy with Christian stitched onto his apron rang me up and thankfully, didn't say anything about my choices, made pleasant small talk and bagged my stuff up.

I practically ran out of there. Maybe it was because Dillon had asked about my future? Maybe it was because Dillon was so... nice? So is the All-American good guy nice?

I wasn't used to that. In L.A. people were nice to me because they wanted something. They wanted me to make them money, they wanted me to appear on their TV shows or Instagram Livestreams.

Had I really been in such rarefied air so long that I'd lost touch with the kinds of people who were just nice for the sake of it?

Whatever the reason, I hurried back to the car and checked into my little motel room as quickly as possible.

Chapter Two
Dillon

Six weeks earlier

"There you go, Dillon," Dad handed the keys to Foggy Basin Grocery to me. "Now it's official."

I took a deep breath. It was only an old keyring with two keys on it, one for the front door and one for the back... but it was the weight of responsibility hitting me.

I was in charge now. The grocery was mine. Mine to manage. Mine to run.

Sure, I'd been working towards this all my life, I knew how the store ran. I knew all the regulars. I'd even taken a business course and read all the books on business I could find... but I was still nervous.

Taking over the family business from my folks was a big deal.

Mom must have seen it in my face, because she hugged me tight. "You'll be great Dillon. And besides, you can always call us if you need to."

"Yeah, I know. Thanks Mom, thanks Dad." I hugged Dad next. They were itching to leave, you could see it in their faces.

Their second-hand motorhome was parked right outside the store ready for them to jump in and drive off into new adventures.

It was bittersweet. I was ready to stand on my own feet of course, taking over the family business was my lifelong dream. But having the two of them leave me alone to do it was frightening all the same.

Still, no one could argue they hadn't earned this. A traveling retirement, driving around the country, seeing all kinds of beautiful sights? They had worked long and hard for this.

"Okay, get out of here already." I put on a brave face for their sake, making a joke of it so they didn't linger until Mom started to tear up.

"Take care of the place, son," Dad slapped me on the shoulder.

My chest filled with something warm. Being trusted, the prospect of my own future... I don't know. I waved them off, and turned to go inside, ready to start the day.

***

Six weeks later

"Another postcard for you!" The mailman handed me a card from the Glacier National Park in Montana. On the back was Mom's familiar handwriting. The same old message *'Having a wonderful time, wish you could see it. I'll send photos when we get some wifi, love you, hope the shop's going well! Make sure you check on Ivy Xoxo Mom and Dad'*

Dillon tacked it up on the pinboard alongside the others, which tracked their progress from southern California.

Christian was running the till, giving me time to take care of the accounts, which were pretty much stable.

I hadn't changed anything besides hiring Christian to help out. I had kept on stocking the same milk, cheese and fresh produce as ever. My suppliers all knew me so they brought all the same things by default. I'd kept the store open by doing the same things.

The locals asked about my parents. I went through the motions of the shop each day. They were familiar routines and there was a comfort in that, but I found now I was in charge, I wanted to shake something up. Just a little.

It was bugging me actually. I wanted to put my own mark on the store, find a way to make more money, and show my parents I could be successful without them. Try something new.

But how?

The idea that had been niggling at me for over a year, ever since I'd been sick in bed and fallen down a YouTube rabbit hole of Korean cooking. Interested, I'd experimented with Korean dishes and got a taste for it, but I had to go to the Asian supermarket two towns over to get supplies like kimchi and cellophane noodles.

I wondered if there would be a market for that, here?

I could dedicate half a fridge to some kimchi, couldn't I?

The locals would love it, wouldn't they?

Heading to the small office, I sat at my dad's desk and booted up the computer. I'd upgraded it for him the year before so that it actually did things like go online, and send emails, unlike the ancient thing he'd been working with.

I went online and looked through the supplier's website, adding some new things to the cart for the delivery later in the week. My heart sped up a little, like I was rebelling for the first time in my life. Sad. Age twenty seven and my first rebellion against my parents was to order gochujang for the store shelf?

Well. Better late than never.

I smiled to myself and clicked 'order'.

"What're you doing?" Ivy appeared at my elbow. "You're grinning like you're getting away with something."

I pressed my hand over my heart. My little sister had a particular knack for walking silently and scaring the crap out of me.

"Ordering something new for the shop," I said.

Ivy shook her head. She was twenty-two and studying post-graduate creative writing at California State University in Sacramento, but she was home on spring break. "I need you to live a little larger, Dill. You're breaking my heart. You never go out, you never meet anyone new, and your entire life is this dang shop."

I laughed, elbowing her to make space so I could tidy up the desk a little. Ivy leaned against the wall in the corner and watched me.

"You're not denying it."

"Why would I?" I shrugged. "I love it here. The shop is the family business, and since you're the baby you get to follow your big dream and be the creative one. I'm happy to take this over and make it my own."

"Okay, fine," she rolled her eyes expressively. "So you're planning on being a bachelor forever?"

I hesitated before answering this one. Of course I wanted a boyfriend, a husband, someone to look after me when I was sick, someone to go out on dates with.

Some small towns were still unkind to gay folks but Foggy Basin wasn't like that. Heck, sometimes it felt like half the town was queer. But that didn't mean I was constantly running into hot guys who wanted to marry a grocer.

"It's not the time for it," I said, making excuses that both of us knew were excuses. "I want to get myself fully settled in here, make sure I'm confident in keeping the business running before I—"

"Before you have some fun?" Ivy sighed. "You're pathetic, Dill. You can't just keep on putting off your own wants and needs forever."

"Well, there's the other stuff as well." I turned to look at Ivy, significantly.

Ivy shook her head. "Autism is far more well understood and accepted these days, Dill. You know that. So you like some things done a certain way, that's not a deal breaker you know. You're a good guy with a steady job and a great heart. The right guy will love you for all of you."

I sat back in the chair and rubbed my hand over my face. "When did you get so wise, Ivy?"

"At college," she said. "I'm a genius, I'll have you know. My tutor reckons my poetry is going to change the world."

Chapter Three

Tane

*T*he day before

"You could change the spelling of your stage name to make it easier to say, easier to remember," Andrew Lane said. It wasn't the first time he'd brought this up, and I had told him absolutely not each and every time. "Make it like F — e — t — o — o?"

I shook my head, even though I knew he couldn't see me. "No, Andrew. It's staying with the correct spelling. W — h — e — t — u."

There was a pause on the other end of the call. "Okay I know you care about this, but how about something us Americans can easily say?"

"It's my culture, my heritage, my name was chosen to reflect that. I'm not going to change it up because you want something easier to say."

"Come on, Tane, you know I don't mean it like that, it's just from a marketing perspective..."

"Next you'll be suggesting I let people call me 'Tayne'."

I rolled my eyes and resisted the urge to hang up on him. He was my manager, I shouldn't do that, but I really, really wanted to.

I looked around the room, searching for something to anchor me, something that would calm me down and stop me biting off this man's head. My guitar? Nah, that had too much emotion associated.

The view out the window of my apartment showed Los Angeles sprawling into the valley. The sky was vast and blue, cloudless like normal.

Part of me really missed winter.

Most of me wanted to escape.

"How about what it means? What does whetu mean again?" Andrew blathered on, oblivious.

"It means star, but I'm not going to go around calling myself star, I'll tell you that for free. I'll sound like an asshole."

"Okay, I'll workshop it with the marketing team and we'll get back to you."

"Don't bother, I'm not going to change my name."

"All right, and I'm working on spin about how long your new album is taking to come out, let me know if you have any statements you'd like included."

I hung up on him.

I dropped my head into my hands and tried to order my thoughts. I had a gig tonight. I had to get myself into the space for it. I had to focus on the music.

It had once been everything I wanted, it had been my escape from the little country at the bottom of the world that I came from. It had been my money maker, my everything.

I thought back with jealousy to how I'd felt when I first came to the States.

Back then, I'd been in love with the act of creation, staying up all night in a creative whirl, writing new scraps of melody, new beats. Show them to people — like my manager — and get hype in return.

Now? It felt hollow.

It felt like something I *had* to do. The joy was long gone. It was work now.

My brain wasn't providing anything new or fun. In fact, in place of new melodies and ideas for lyrics, my brain was static. The sound of a speaker when a guitar has been plugged in but no one's strumming.

Nothing but white noise.

Groaning, I picked up my phone. Andrew wouldn't call back, he'd be off with marketing by now, I was sure.

There was a disturbing number of new notifications. On my Instagram, on my incoming messages, on email. Looking at the numbers made my mind go blank.

They wanted to know why I'd pushed the release date of my new album back. I'd done it three times. I couldn't very well keep them hanging... but I had barely written anything I could use for an album either.

There was too much pressure. I couldn't think of anything except the gripping fear that took hold of me as those numbers ticked up, even as I was looking at them.

Static played riotous in my head. Nothing but white noise, roaring too loud in my ear.

I had to get away.

That's all there was to it. I'd do that night's gig like normal, pack all the shit I cared about and hire a car, and be gone in the morning.

But go where?

I couldn't just fly home, I wasn't ready for that. Ma would have so many questions, and I didn't have answers. Besides, it would involve too much paperwork, then a twelve hour flight. Nope. Too-hard basket.

I had to go somewhere no one would know who I was — which wouldn't be too hard outside of L.A., San Francisco and New York City. I was only really big on the club scenes, and in Japan. And I wasn't about to fly to Japan, same issues with flying home. Too much admin.

Ignoring the little bubbles of numbers, I opened an accommodation app that I used fairly regularly. There had to be something...

I tapped filters. Hotel or motel, yeah that was fine. No shared accommodation AirBnB bs. I wanted my own bathroom, thank you very much.

Somewhere within a day's drive.

Somewhere not a city.

There were a lot of options. I hadn't really realised there were so many small towns in California.

I slumped back on the plush cushions of my couch and opened Instagram instead. I ignored the notifications and scrolled. I followed a lot of travel influencers and one of them had posted a gorgeous picture of a small town. Where was it?

Foggy Basin.

I clicked on the location tag. It checked all the boxes.

I looked up accommodation and booked a room at the local motel without even thinking about it.

Done. For tonight.

This was really happening. I stood up, feeling briefly light-headed but mostly... euphoric.

I was taking control.

Escaping.

Taking my life into my own hands before I was smothered by everything. All the things people needed from me piled onto my back like a dead weight and I couldn't take it anymore. I was sinking, quicksand sucking me down.

It was time to pack.

Chapter Four

Dillon

The next day I was tidying the cereal shelves when I saw Tane walk into the store again. I'd seen him purchase two boxes of cereal and a whole lot of junk food the day before.

I didn't know who this guy was, or what had brought him to our little down for an undetermined amount of time, but I was damned if I'd let him walk out with nothing but simple carbohydrates and high-fructose cornstarch again.

I walked briskly to intercept him. He looked up at me, startled. His brown eyes caused something to catch in my chest. His eyelashes were so long and his eyebrows perfectly sculpted. I didn't even know I cared about eyebrows but his? They were perfection.

"Might I interest you in our store-packed meals for one?" I said, as smoothly as I could.

Tane's perfect eyebrows shot up. "Uh, your what now?"

"I couldn't help but notice yesterday, your choices were somewhat unhealthy." I took him gently by the elbow and directed him to the refrigerated shelves by the back wall, where we stocked salads, roast meals ready to reheat, filled rolls and charcuterie board packs.

Tane didn't resist being guided. He made a sort of amused grunt and breathed out when he saw the spread before him.

"You noticed what I bought?"

"Well, yes." I realized, too late, that it might come across as strange and vaguely stalker-like. "I just... pay attention to stock here, it's my job. I don't want you to get sick from only eating snacks and stuff, maybe consider something... more real?"

"More real," Tane echoed. He was definitely laughing at me now. "I came here from L.A. I'd have to go to a Wholefoods and pay twenty bucks for a salad to get something real there. Or Nobu for the most expensive sushi this side of Japan."

I relaxed, glad he was amused and not entirely alienated. "We don't have prices like that here," I said.

"I'm sure you don't."

"So, you'll try something with a fresh vegetable in it?"

"Now you sound like one of my aunties," Tane laughed.

He tugged away from me and I was shocked to realize I'd been holding his elbow this entire time. How had I just kept hold of him? That was weird. I was being so weird.

I stepped back a little. "The turkey roll is particularly good. These are all made for us by a local, they supply them fresh every morning."

Tane picked up a turkey roll and a salad, plus a little cheese and cracker pack. "Thanks for the suggestion, I appreciate it. I guess I'm not really used to taking care of myself..." he trailed off.

But dang if that didn't pique my interest. I knew better than to pry though. But I'd already insinuated myself into his day. Why had I done that? Why was I acting so familiar with him? It wasn't like me.

I mean I was used to small town life, you kinda ended up knowing everything about everyone who lived in Foggy Basin, but with strangers? I usually kept a considered, professional distance.

But something about Tane...

"You know we also have lots of great produce and stuff, if you want to cook from scratch?" I couldn't help myself. I was compulsive. I wanted this man to eat well and look after himself, and I didn't know why except it had something to do with his eyebrows.

"Oh uh, yeah I saw that," Rane said. "I don't really... It's been a long time since I cooked anything for myself. I think I've forgotten how."

A terrible impulse reared up inside me. I knew it was a mistake but I couldn't help it. Before I could run away, I blurted, "I'll cook for you if you like? How about you come to my place for dinner?"

My face immediately burned red and I opened my mouth to take it back.

Tane's eyebrows quirked up. "For real?"

I nodded. "Yeah it's... you know. Small town hospitality."

Tane sucked on his lower lip, apparently considering, then he smiled and shook his head. "Nah, it's okay. Thanks though, it's really nice of you to offer but I'll be fine."

I swallowed down an unreasonable amount of disappointment. "Okay well, if you change your mind you know where to find me."

Tane nodded and headed off down the aisle, no doubt entirely freaked out by the random offer of a home cooked meal by a guy he'd known for all of three minutes.

Running my hands through my hair, I berated myself for acting so weird. I couldn't even blame it on my Autism, I was simply acting strangely. Something about Tane had me off-footed. I wanted to look after him? Weird urge.

When I dropped my arms, Ivy grabbed me, startling me again.

She spoke in an urgent whisper. "Dill. Was that...Whetu?"

"No, his name's Tane." I whispered back, not wanting to be overheard.

Her fingernails dug into my arm. "Whetu is a stage name. Tane is his real name. Oh my fucking god, is it really him? You were touching him!"

"What are you talking about?"

"Only the biggest up and coming star of club R&B right now."

I turned to look Ivy in the eyes, sure she was messing with me, but she stared right back, certain as anything.

"What, you're saying he's famous?"

Ivy let go of my arm. "Yes, exceptionally, he's brilliant, and he's here? Why is he here?"

"I don't know," I rubbed my arm, sure she'd have bruised it. "He said he's here for maybe a week, but he was very vague."

"Maybe he's writing his new album and he knew nothing here would distract him, since this town is dull as dishwater." Ivy went up on her tip toes, tracking Tane around the shop. "I'm going to go and tell him how wonderful he is."

I grabbed her arm. "No, you're not. He's obviously here for his own reasons and if you make a fuss of him, he might leave." Ivy stared at me. "You know, leave without buying anything," I finished, weakly.

The idea of spooking Tane frightened me. I didn't want to do anything that could possibly make him feel uncomfortable.

For whatever reason, I wanted him to like it here. To like the town.

Ivy racing over there and blowing his cover by fangirling over all of him would be the opposite of that. She glanced in the direction he'd gone and then her shoulders slumped. "Fine. I'll leave him alone, but I'm bringing one of his LPs with me tomorrow in case he comes in again."

"Don't you have some homework to do?" I pushed her gently towards the backroom.

"Yeah."

I looked back as I hustled her into the back and saw Tane was chatting with Christian as he checked out his purchases. He looked relaxed.

I was way too relieved.

Tane

I sat on a park bench to eat and enjoy a little sunshine.

The turkey roll was objectively great. Easy access to turkey as a deli meat was one of the great small joys of living in the States. Back home turkeys were farmed pretty minimally, so it was definitely a once-a-year special occasion treat.

But this roll? Wholemeal bread, layers of turkey, salad greens, the perfect amount of mayo? It was exactly what I needed.

I sent a silent thank you to Dillon.

Not too far from me a young man started busking with a violin. He wasn't bad. I wondered what his plan was, he couldn't have been eighteen yet, but did he have a big music career planned? Something like mine?

I tore my eyes away from him and looked back at my sandwich. I didn't want to think about music right then. Dillon with the dreamy blue eyes and warm smile was a much more comforting thing to daydream about.

I wondered what he'd meant by asking me to dinner? Was he just being friendly or was he coming onto me? I dismissed the thought. In a small town like this, there was no chance anyone here was gay, right?

I finished up my sandwich, tossed the rubbish into the nearest bin and walked slowly back up Main Street to my little motel room.

Being away from L.A. was a relief, but in all honestly, I was starting to get sort of bored. I picked up my guitar on a whim. It was the usual thing to do, the thing that comforted me, that rooted me to the ground... but I could barely bring myself to put my fingers on the frets.

I froze, my heart thudding with urgency and my breath restricting in my chest.

I couldn't do it.

There was nothing in my head but white noise and a voice shouting 'no!'

I put the guitar back in its case. I shouldn't have even brought it with me.

Lying back on the bed I flicked the TV on some melodramatic made-for-TV movie and tried to forget about everything.

Taking care of my basic needs: food, water, rest... those would be what I spent my energy on for the foreseeable future.

Chapter Five

Dillon

When I saw Tane come into the shop the next day and head straight for the refrigerated foods I felt my shoulders relax. Some part of me had been worried I'd scared Tane off for good, and seeing him again eased that stress.

I was busy serving Evelyn, and trying to maintain my conversation with her, but my attention was on Tane.

"All those young men moving in," she said. "That gaming company, Queen's Ransom or whatever it is, I don't know what it'll do to the town."

"Queen Gaming," I said. "It'll be nice to have some new blood, don't you think?"

Evelyn pursed her lips, a sparkle in her eyes. "You're eyeing some of them up, aren't you? It's about time you settled down with someone, you know. Had some kids maybe, now that you've taken over the family business."

This was such a turn in the conversation that my cheeks flamed hot. "Evelyn, I don't think—"

"Now, don't be shy with me," she said. "I've known you since you were a baby, and I know your parents want grandchildren."

I swallowed, my throat dry. My gaze skittered from her and around the shop. The worst would be if some of the guys working for Queen Gaming were in right now, hearing this. Evelyn would probably try and get us married on the spot. Thankfully it was quiet, just me, Evelyn and of course... Tane.

He was so obviously listening to this conversation, a smile playing around his mouth. He caught me looking and ducked behind a display of steel-cut oats.

"Uh, well... of course, I'd like to someday..." I managed to stutter. "I'm waiting for mister right."

"Well, maybe you could get on that Flamer app and see if any of them are the right one."

"Flamer?"

Evelyn paid and hefted her bag on one hip. "That app for gay men."

She seemed to be speaking louder and louder. The last two words echoed through the store.

"Uh... Tinder?" my voice was barely a gasp.

"That's the one!"

I heard a muffled giggle from the breakfast foods.

"Maybe." I cleared my throat. "Thanks, Evelyn, it's always a pleasure."

She nodded, catching sight of someone walking past outside. "Oh, there's Sheriff Clay, I did mean to talk to him about —"

I didn't hear what she wanted to talk to the sheriff about, as she hurried out the shop to flag him down.

Tane sidled up to the counter, setting an armful of food down on the counter. "She was a hard case, eh?"

Tane's New Zealand accent threw me for a moment, but then I worked out what he was saying.

"Yeah, Evelyn knows everything about everyone."

"Just like my aunty," Tane nodded.

He had a really nice smile, it crinkled his eyes. His lips looked so soft, so full...

I was staring at his lips.

That definitely counted as weird.

I was losing the thread of the conversation. "Your aunty?" I managed to say, tearing my eyes from his lips. "You mentioned multiple aunties before I think?"

"Yeah, they're not all my actual blood aunties," Tane said. "Just like, women who've been there all my life, mum's friends, that kind of thing. They love to know what's going on and give their opinions freely."

I chuckled. "My parents are both only children, so it was really just us. My folks, my sister and me."

"Nice." Tane handed me his card and I rang him up.

"Good to see you're eating things with vegetables in," I said. The need to take care of him flared up again. Maybe because he'd mentioned his aunties and I imagined him back in New Zealand surrounded by people? Maybe because I wanted to taste his lips? But it flared up and I asked him again, sure he'd turn me down. "The offer is open, if you want to come over for a home-cooked meal some time."

Tane blinked at me. I ducked my head and bagged his groceries.

"Thanks," he said. "But I couldn't impose on you, I just bought all this, after all." He was joking, but not in a nasty way. He was making a joke of it so I didn't freak out over being rejected.

"Of course," I said. "Well, you know where I am if you change your mind."

"That I do. Take care, eh?" Tane gave me a little wave and left with his bag of food.

Ivy came in not ten minutes later with her vinyl of Whetu's work.

"You just missed him," I said. "The man himself."

"Aw, boo." Ivy stuck her lower lip out dramatically. "Can I leave this here for when he comes back?"

She made like she was going to slide it in next to the till. "No! Someone will want to buy it or something, besides it's too big and it sticks out. Put it in the back if you really have to leave it."

Ivy rolled her eyes and went in the back.

The next day Christian was on the till when Tane came in. Tane looked tired. More than he had been any other day. He looked worn out.

My heart went out to him.

I figured the third time might be the charm and intercepted him on the way towards the take-and-bake pizzas.

"Hey, Tane," I said.

His face lit up when he saw me. "Hey Dillon, you're like, always here, aren't you?"

"Well, it is my business..." I said.

"No hobbies or anything?"

"Uhm, well... not really," I said. "I'm kind of boring to be honest. I sometimes go jogging, and I like to cook?"

Tane's eyebrow raised.

I felt like some kind of lothario but I couldn't help myself, I wanted to get to know him better and the only way to do that would be outside of my place of business.

"I didn't even mean for that to be a segue, but I did want to bring up the idea of dinner with you one more time. I know you're just visiting but I don't like, see you out and about a lot so I thought maybe you're a bit lonely?" I remembered what he'd said the day before. "It's no imposition. I'll cook something healthy but delicious. What do you say?"

Tane sucked his lower lip for a moment, his expression unreadable, then he broke into a warm smile.

"Yeah, okay. That sounds nice."

Relief flooded me, he didn't think it was weird, or if he did, he didn't care. He wanted to come over.

"Okay um, well, how about you come back round at closing time tonight and I'll... cook for us?" I was instantly planning menus, trying to decide which would be best.

Tane nodded. "Great, thanks, man. Do you drink? I can bring some bottles of something?"

"Yes, I drink. You don't have to bring anything though, it's on me."

Tane chuckled. "No, my mother taught me never to go to someone's place empty-handed."

I could understand that. "Okay then, whatever you like will be fine."

"Great." Tane grinned at me. "Well, I'd better find something to bring then."

"Oh uh, my place is just upstairs, but take my number as well, in case you're running late or something?"

Tane produced a brand new Samsung phone and opened the messaging app, he handed me the phone. "Put your number in there and I'll text you so you have mine."

I did as he said, punching in my numbers and then handing it back to him. A moment later my phone vibrated in my pocket.

"I guess I'll drop by at closing time?"

"Perfect." I nodded. "See you then."

Tane left the store, and I went into the backroom, holding it together long enough to be out of sight of the shop before bending in half to have a mild panic reaction.

I screwed my eyes shut and gripped my knees, focusing on taking breaths in from my belly. There was nothing to worry about. It was just dinner. I could make dinner.

It was just dinner I was making for a really cute foreigner who, oh yeah, just happened to be a global phenomenon in music.

What was I thinking?

More to the point, what would I make?

I heaved in a raspy breath and forced myself back upright. I could do this. There was nothing to panic about. All I had to do was cook something edible and not be a complete weirdo.

Totally doable, right?

Chapter Six

Tane

I was due at the grocery shop in a half hour, I'd already showered and the bottles of beer I'd bought were waiting in a bag by the door of my motel room.

I was weirdly nervous. It felt so intimate to go to Dillon's house, but I did believe he had invited me as a friendly gesture, not out of some weird sense of obligation.

With nothing much else to do, I went on my phone and looked up my own Instagram. I didn't sign in, I didn't want to see the flood of DMs, but there were comments I could read on my latest post. The one I made when I was still in L.A.

Even looking up my Whetu branded social media created a knot in my stomach. How could I ever even go back to touring if I couldn't even look at a picture?

The comments were full of concern: *Where are you? I miss your updates Hope you're not sick, please feel better soon*

I closed the window down and sighed. What was I going to do?

I'd run away from my entire life... Now what?

Should I just head back to Aotearoa?

And face up to all my disappointed aunties and cousins?

That made the knot in my stomach even worse.

I opened up my banking app. At least I had plenty of cash... if I wanted to head home I could, no problem. I could head anywhere in the world. Move to somewhere no one would ever look for me. Rural Japan? Norway? Some little island in the Pacific like Rarotonga? I laughed off that last one. Rarotonga was the number one tourist destination for New Zealanders. I'd be found in a matter of weeks.

I stood up and looked out the window at the town limits close by. Or here? No one would look for me here. I'd chosen Foggy Basin in such a random way, it was a cute town but it was basically a nothing town as well. There must be hundreds of towns just like it.

Groaning, I turned away from the window and rubbed my stomach. I didn't need to decide anything now. I just had to go meet Dillon and eat some dinner. That's all I had to do.

On a whim, that I was certain I'd regret, I picked up my guitar and slung it over my back. I grabbed the beers on my way out the door and walked slowly towards the grocer's.

The evening was another mild one. Not too hot, not cold, just pleasant and mild. The sun was headed towards the horizon and I looked around with new eyes.

Could I live here?

Would the quiet get to me after so long in a big city?

I simply didn't know the answers.

Dillon locked up the shop just as I approached. "Hey Tane, good timing!"

"Good evening!" I called.

He led the way to the upstairs apartment. The inside was incredibly neat and tidy. It made my situation at the motel feel extra seedy, since they'd only provided two drawers and a tiny wardrobe, so I was mostly living out of my suitcase and a pile on a chair.

"Come in, make yourself comfortable," Dillon said. "I put dinner in the slow cooker this morning so it won't take long to prepare once you're hungry."

"In the meantime..." I handed him the bag of beers. "I couldn't find any New Zealand beers, but these should be fine."

I blushed a little, I'd just implied that there would definitely be a next time, which was presumptuous of me.

Dillon smiled and took the bag. "Thank you. Do you want a glass? Or just out of the bottle?"

"Out of the bottle is fine." I set my guitar carefully down in the corner and took a seat as Dillon cracked open the beer then handed it to me.

"I'll join you." He opened one for himself and sat down. "Busy day?"

I shook my head. "Not at all. I'm gonna be honest with you, I'm kind of spinning my wheels at the moment."

Dillon's gaze cut to my guitar in the corner. "You play?"

"Yeah I'm..." I figured it was time to come clean. I was in his house, sharing a beer, he was about to feed me. If we weren't friends already we were about to be. "I'm a musician. But, I'm on a break at the moment."

Dillon smiled, not a single bit of surprise registered on his face. "Oh yeah?"

"You knew." I narrowed my eyes at him.

"Well, my little sister, she recognised you. She's a big fan. I had to banish her to a friend's tonight or she'd have forced you to sign every album you've ever released."

I took a deep drink of my beer then had to laugh. "Thanks for sparing me from that, then?"

"I mean, there's only so much I can do. I've spared you for this evening, but it's a small town, she'll track you down eventually."

I laughed again and rubbed my face. "You're probably right about that."

"For what it's worth, I wouldn't have any idea who you are if it wasn't for her," Dillon said. "But I looked up some of your music and I like it. We don't have to talk about it tonight though."

"Thanks, it's all a bit of a tender area for me right now," I said.

Honesty again. What was it about Dillon that was so disarming? I felt so comfortable with him, so at home. I knew he wouldn't judge, and more than that... I knew he wouldn't lie to me. There was nothing about him that read 'player'. He'd be eaten alive in L.A. I wasn't used to being around someone who inspired the truth. It was a vulnerable sensation. I sipped my beer again, hoping I didn't stick my foot in it somehow.

"Of course."

"How was the store today?" I asked, a nice safe topic of conversation.

Dillon's shoulders relaxed — he'd been nervous too? — and he told me about his day.

His voice was deep and soothing, I realised he could be telling me the most boring details about adding up his finances and I'd be invested. I actually tuned out of what he was really saying, just letting myself drift on the calm ocean of his voice, until he stopped and looked at me quizzically.

"Uh, sorry what?" I sat up straighter.

Dillon chuckled. "I'm going to make dinner up, you're welcome to stay here and chill or you can come help, it's up to you."

"I'll help." I followed him into the kitchen. "Although my cooking skills are pretty basic."

The kitchen smelled incredible, something savoury that made my stomach rumble.

"I made chili, so we can eat it with nacho chips and stuff if you like?" Dillon seemed uncertain all of a sudden.

"Nachos sound great," I nodded. "Do you have avocados? I think I can be trusted to make guacamole."

"Right there." He pointed at the chopping board and a bowl of avocados.

We worked alongside each other in companionable silence and a calm settled over me. I wasn't anxious, I wasn't nervous, instead I felt … at home.

It was a dangerous feeling, one that I couldn't begin to trust. There were a million and one reasons why I couldn't be reading too much into this evening. I had no idea what my future was, for one.

So I just tried to relax, humming something to myself, some old song from back home and Dillon worked quietly.

Dillon

Making dinner together with Tane and then eating it across from each other at the kitchen table had me feeling some kind of way. I knew there was no possible chance that a big-time musician from the other side of the world would ever consider dating me, let alone move into a small town and become the supermarket boss's husband… but I couldn't help dreaming about it.

He was softly spoken, gentle with his words as if he considered each one before he said it.

His eyelashes were criminally long, black and fluttering over his rich brown eyes. I wanted to cup his cheek and feel how soft his skin was, even with the five o'clock shadow. I wanted to know everything about him.

More than anything, I wanted him to be mine.

I realised I was staring and cleared my throat. "So, what brought you here, to Foggy Basin?"

Tane's gentle smile faded and a furrow appeared between his eyebrows. I wished with all my heart I could take back the question that had given him even a tiny amount of distress.

"Ah, just... needed to get away," he waved his hand vaguely. "So, you said you have a little sister?"

I recognised the deflection and accepted it immediately. "Yeah, she's studying, she's a writer. Ivy. She's kind of my everything, you know? Our parents are really great, they raised us right and everything. But I've always been pretty happy to stay in my lane, do the expected thing. Ivy's like a wild creature who could never be controlled." I blushed, realised I was gushing about my own sister and bit my lip. "Have you got siblings?"

Tane shook his head. "Nah, my folks split when I was little and Ma raised me. She never dated anyone else, said she was done with it. I have a lot of cousins though, both blood and not."

"They must be really proud of you," I blurted. I shouldn't have done that, he immediately ducked his head. "Sorry, you don't want to talk about work and I keep circling back to it. Just ignore me."

Tane smiled, his eyes crinkling. "Thanks. For understanding."

"Have you had enough to eat? I didn't make dessert or anything but there's probably puddings in the cupboard?"

Tane shook his head. "Nah, this was really good though thanks. I appreciated all the vegetables in the chili."

"Let's move to the couches then." As we stood up, Tane started stacking the plates like he was going to bus them. "I'll do the dishes later, leave them."

Back in the living room the silence stretched out again. I was right about to ask him about New Zealand when he picked up his guitar. "Mind if I play something?"

I could barely breathe. He was being so damned romantic. "I'd love that."

Damn me and my not being able to conceal anything. I blushed and he chuckled as he sat, checking the tuning on the guitar. He held the guitar as if it was a precious object, and for all I knew it was. I didn't know the first thing about musical instruments, or what was expensive.

He cleared his throat, hesitated for a moment, then started to strum.

I nodded a little, feeling the rhythm, but I stopped moving altogether when he started to sing. His low speaking voice transformed into a pure, dreamy tenor as he sang in a language I didn't recognise, but could guess was Māori.

It was a sweet, lilting song, yearning but infinitely pretty. I wondered desperately what it meant, transfixed by his voice, and the open way he held my gaze. Any shyness I'd seen from him previously was entirely gone, lost in the confidence of his beautiful singing voice.

He smiled, and I saw the way it played across his features. At the pinnacle of the song he raised his voice loud and fine, filling my apartment with the notes and tears prickled my eyes.

I quickly grabbed the dregs of my beer and downed them, trying to create distance from the emotions he was drawing out of me. I swiped at my eyes and swallowed hard.

He finished with a last strum and I set my bottle down to applaud him.

"Tane, that was incredible!"

"Ah, it's okay. It's a song I grew up with, everyone back home knows it." He was deflecting, acting like what he'd done was nothing special. I leaned forward on my knees and shook my head.

"No, you were amazing. Your voice is so pure! So pretty!"

Tane chuckled and strummed the guitar again. "Thank you."

Something surged inside me, a desperate need. I wanted to go to him. I wanted to move the guitar aside, sit in his lap and kiss him hard. I gripped the couch cushions to stop myself moving. I didn't know what his preferences were, and I'd invited him over like this to be friendly, to offer a tiny bit of community.

I cleared my throat. "So um, do you have a girlfriend?"

Tane lifted his head to answer and we both heard the clatter of someone coming up the stairs. My stomach sank. Ivy had ignored me and come home even though she knew I'd asked her not to.

"That'll be Ivy," I said. "I'm sorry..."

"It's fine." In an instant Tane had packed his guitar into its case and was standing up. "I should be heading back anyway. This was wonderful, thank you for the meal, Dill. I really appreciate it."

I stood up, accompanying him to the door. A wild, desperate part of me wanted him to kiss me goodnight, but the door opened just as we approached.

Ivy stood there, dishevelled, her eyes red with tears, or something like it.

"Catch you later," Tane waved and sidled past Ivy.

"Goodnight!" I called out, reaching for my sister. "What's up?"

"Ah just stupid stuff," Ivy sounded like she was annoyed, and didn't want to talk, but she also shoved herself bodily into my chest. "Sorry for ruining your night."

I wrapped my arms around her, frowning. "You didn't. What's going on, Ivy, you look like you've been crying."

Ivy shook her head and hugged me tight for a moment before letting go. She swiped her sleeve over her eyes.

"It's fine. Just a weird night, is all. I'll be okay, I'll just go to bed."

"Did you eat? There's leftover chili if you want it."

But Ivy was already heading to her room. "I'm fine, don't worry about me!" She closed the door forcefully.

Telling me not to worry when she'd turned up out of the blue and looking upset had the exact opposite effect. But I knew not to try and follow her, not right away anyway.

I busied myself with cleaning up the dishes from dinner, packing away the leftovers and cleaning the kitchen. Once that was all done I made up a hot cocoa and went to her door. Knocking gently on the door I called out. "Ivy, I made you cocoa..."

She opened the door a moment later. She looked a lot more relaxed, and accepted the drink with a smile. "Thanks, big bro. Broseph. My elder, my hyung..."

Relieved, I laughed too, if she was making stupid jokes I knew whatever had happened couldn't have been too bad.

"I'm here, any time you want to talk, you know that right?"

Ivy wrapped her hands around the mug and nodded. "Yeah. I know. When there's something to talk about I'll come right to you, promise."

"Okay. Goodnight, then."

I still felt a little uneasy, but I left her to it.

Chapter Seven

Tane

The next few days I visited the grocery store every day, saying hi to Dillon if he was around, chatting with Christian, his assistant and I even agreed to sign Ivy's vinyl for her, although I did it as covertly as possible. It wouldn't do to have other people notice me.

I had a little routine going, sitting on the same park bench to have a snack. Walking up and down Main Street, visiting the various shops. I even picked up some books and tried reading them.

In the evenings, I managed to fool around a little with my guitar. Doing it in front of Dillon seemed to have unlocked the block I'd been having over music. I didn't make anything groundbreaking, or even particularly interesting, but I was having fun with it. I couldn't remember the last time I'd made music just for the fun of it, without thinking about if it would be marketable or not.

I ate out a couple of nights but there were really only two restaurants, and the premade sandwiches were great but I liked hot food in the evening.

Finally, I got up the courage to ask Dillon if he'd allow me to cook something for him. I'd done the necessary preparation for what I wanted to make, and the time was right.

It was awkward, because of course there was no stove or oven at the motel, so I was basically inviting myself over to his house, but we'd been friendly ever since I'd run out of his apartment in a panic.

That evening had got intense somehow, but it was in a good way. A frightening way, but good. I wasn't sure what might have happened if Ivy hadn't shown up.

It was Saturday when I managed to grab Dillon. "Hey, um, I wanted to repay you for dinner the other night. I'm not much of a cook but I thought I could make something Kiwi for you."

"Kiwi?" Dillon's eyes cut to the fruit and vegetable section. "Kiwi as in the bird, not the fruit. It's what we call ourselves, in Aotearoa, although I don't know why. It's a stupid, round flightless bird, but there you have it."

I bit my tongue. I was babbling.

Babbling! Like a nervous teenager chatting up his crush.

"Oh! That would be wonderful, thank you," Dillon said after a moment. I guessed he'd needed the time to parse what I'd been babbling about.

"The thing is, I'd need to use your kitchen for it," I said.

"Sure, of course." Dillon nodded. "I'm here until six again but if you want to head up earlier, I think Ivy is there. She might join us, I don't know if she has plans or anything." Something flickered across his face, concern maybe, and I remembered how Ivy had looked upset the other night.

"Is she okay?"

Dillon's smile only lifted one side of his mouth. "I think so. I don't really know what's going on there. She'll be over the moon to spend time with you, though."

I smiled, mentally bracing myself. "Okay, well, if it's okay then I can head over this afternoon and get things started?"

Dillon took a breath. "It's... the kitchen is... I like how it's organised. Can you please be sure and return everything to the place you've found it when you're done?"

I nodded. "Yes, of course I will. You can trust me. I'll just pick up a few things first."

Dillon breathed out heavily. "I'll text Ivy and let her know to expect you, and again. I'm sorry in advance."

Laughing, I waved off his apology. "I've dealt with fans before, Dillon, I'm sure it will be fine."

I went to collect the ingredients I needed — while I was sure Dillon would have some of them in his kitchen, I didn't want to risk messing things up with rooting through his supplies. Better to take new ones and contain the chaos. I wasn't super confident with many dishes, but I was going to make some old favourites, and I was sure I'd impress him.

Trying not to think too hard about *why* I wanted to impress him so much, I took my groceries, collected a couple of things from the motel room and then made my way to Dillon's.

I knocked on the door and Ivy opened it almost immediately.

"HI! Come on in, it's so nice to meet you. Dillon said you'd be cooking dinner? That's so cool, I can help if you like, I'm not really doing anything and I'm pretty okay in the kitchen, you know?"

I set the bags and my guitar down and looked Ivy in the eyes. "Ivy. Thank you, please breathe."

"Breathe? What? I am breathing, I'm totally fine with global superstar recording artist Whetu being in my house."

She fanned herself with one hand.

I gently but firmly took hold of her shoulders. "I'll answer any questions you have, just please, take a breath in and let it out slowly. I don't want you passing out."

"Oh, okay." Ivy took a few slow breaths and her shoulders relaxed under my hands.

I let go.

"You can call me Tane," I said. "Now, what do you want to know?"

Ivy peppered me with the basic questions I was used to getting in interviews, as I gathered things up and we walked together into the kitchen. I answered with as much honesty as I could muster.

Once those questions were out of the way, she relaxed a bit more.

"Thank you for that," she said. "So um, if you don't mind me asking, why the hell are you in Foggy Basin?"

I chuckled as I pulled out the rēwena bug and started measuring flour.

"Wait, before you answer, what the hell is that?"

"It's a rēwena bug? Think like a sourdough starter, but it's for Māori bread. Really I should have made the dough last night and let it rise but... I don't have bowls and stuff at the motel."

Ivy started sorting the rest of my groceries, finding an onion. "Should I chop this?"

"Please." I swallowed, mixing the bug in with water and a little sugar. "You asked why I'm here? I don't know why I chose this town in particular, but it all got too much back in L.A. I felt like I couldn't breathe, everyone just wanted so much, like they were in this massive crowd, yelling and reaching for me and I was standing there, shaking with nothing left to give."

"Ooof." Ivy nodded. "That's a lot."

"So much."

"Has it been better since you've been here?"

I laughed, unable to stop myself. "Yes. Like, I can remember how overwhelmed I was, how my head ached, and if I even think about turning on my old phone I get heart palpitations, but everything is so quiet here. I'm actually sleeping close to seven hours a night, it's so quiet."

"Ugh, tell me about it." Ivy pulled a face. "It's too quiet for me, sometimes. A lot of the time. Glad for you though."

"What are you studying?" I found myself liking Ivy, she was so easy to talk to. Like Dillon, she had a whole aura of *safe* around her that I relaxed into.

"I'm a writer, so I'm studying literature and journalism, but I really want to get into writing and publishing novels," she said.

"What kind of novels?"

"I don't know... I'm still working that part out."

I'd mixed the dough and floured the countertop to turn it out and start kneading it. "So, does your brother have someone special in his life?"

Ivy laughed. "Smooth, very smooth and casual. No, he's single. He's dated before but nothing serious, and yes he's very gay."

I grinned at her, working the dough with muscle memory. She grinned back, and then something about her experience grew troubled.

"Listen, if you're not going to stay in town, please don't mess around with him? He's not as tough and together as he looks, and I don't know what he'd do with a broken heart."

Biting on my lower lip, I nodded. "Yeah, I hear that."

"I don't mean to assume, although you weren't exactly subtle just now."

"I've been thinking about it," I admitted. "It would be nice to have someone as... stable as him in my life. But I really don't know what my plans are. I'll be careful, I promise. Just friends."

"Thanks." Ivy went to set the table.

She was sweet, looking out for him like that. I wondered what had happened to upset her the other night, and wondered if I could ask. We were apparently being straight up with each other, which I appreciated. When she came back into the kitchen, I figured I might as well ask.

"Are you okay, after the other night?" "Hmm? Oh yeah." Ivy's voice lacked expression when she replied, not convincing at all. "I'm just going through some... I dunno, I guess you could call it questioning."

"Want to talk about it?"

She shook her head. "Nah, still processing things. Thanks though."

She excused herself soon after and left me to cook. I put on some lofi music on my phone and lost myself in the simple art of cooking, thinking only of what my hands were doing, and sending thanks to my grandmother for teaching me this recipe.

Dillon

Nervousness fluttered through my chest as I locked up for the day and headed home. I knew Tane meant well, and I was touched that he wanted to return the favour like this, it'd be nice not having to cook for myself. But I was also unreasonably worried that I'd return to find my kitchen messy, not just messy but destroyed.

Okay, maybe I had some trust issues... or control issues. Ivy had said something like that to me before. But things being out of place just rankled. I couldn't concentrate until it was set right again. I hoped beyond hope that Tane had stuck to his word and kept things neat. I knew I couldn't relax and enjoy dinner if I knew there were ingredients and dirty dishes left strewn around.

It was a silly thing to worry about, but knowing that didn't make it any less stressful.

I slowed down on the walk home, taking my time, delaying the inevitable.

Letting myself into the apartment, I was immediately greeted by the most delicious smell imaginable — baking bread. Warm, sweet and the epitome of homey. A knot in my stomach unravelled.

"I'm back!" I called out.

"Welcome home!" Ivy poked her head out of the living room. "Table's all set."

"Hope you're hungry!" Tane called from the kitchen.

"Thanks Ivy." I gave her shoulder a squeeze and went to the kitchen. My fears had been for nothing. Tane had the place nearly spotless. There were pans and things draining on the drying rack, the countertop was clean and a beautiful round loaf of bread was steaming on a chopping board. On another chopping board, something steamed under a tent of tinfoil. There was a small saucepan bubbling on the stovetop. Gravy? My stomach rumbled, all knots gone in favour of a voracious need to eat.

Tane grinned at me and pulled a tray of roast vegetables out of the oven. They smelled great too, but it was all overwhelmed by the bread smell. My mouth watered.

"You made bread?"

Tane set the hot tray on a trivet and gave me a shy smile. "Yeah, it's Māori bread, kind of like a sour dough but better. Go sit down, I'll bring it all out in a minute."

I did as he said, moving through to sit at the table. Ivy sat beside me. She beamed and leaned close to murmur. "I'm staying for dinner, then I'm headed out, don't do anything I wouldn't do..."

I blushed. Even with my little sister here, the lengths Tane had gone to really made this feel like a date. I shook out my napkin and spread it over my lap.

Tane brought out a serving dish with sliced roast lamb, roast potatoes and sweet potato and a chopping board of the sliced bread.

"Roast lamb is really part of the England settler history of Aotearoa," Tane said, setting it down on the table. "And I can't get proper Kumara here, but sweet potatoes are close enough, that's a Māori import. So, uh, yeah, enjoy." He sat down, ducking his head like he was shy about the bounty he'd set out.

"Holy crap, Tane." Ivy shook her head.

I stood up and started serving out the slices of lamb. Ivy took the serving spoon and dished out the roast veges.

"Oh the gravy!" Tane sprung up and hurried back into the kitchen. For all the world reminding me of a fifties housewife in an old sitcom. It was absolutely adorable.

He came back a moment later with the gravy in the gravy boat I'd inherited from my grandmother and offered it around.

"Thank you, really, this is so much and it all looks incredible."

"Dig in," Tane said. "I hope you like it, the bread especially..."

We all started to eat. It was absolutely delicious and I told Tane so after every single bite. The lamb was perfectly cooked, a little rare in the centre and delicately flavoured with rosemary and mint.

"It's like a standard Sunday dinner back home." Tane buttered another piece of rēwena and passed it to me. "But I'm really glad you're enjoying it."

With small talk and more food than I technically needed to consume, the dinner passed very pleasantly. True to her word, after helping to tidy up, Ivy excused herself to go out.

"Hot drink?"

Tane nodded. "Sounds great."

"Tea, coffee, cocoa?"

Tane groaned softly. "Cocoa, oh my God, yes."

I chuckled and made us two cocoas, bringing them to the living room where Tane was relaxing on one end of the couch. He looked up at me and I swallowed, his eyelashes caught my attention again. I really wanted to touch him, to kiss him.

I set the drinks down and sat on the couch near him. He shifted to be closer to me.

What was going to happen?

"That was a really wonderful dinner, thank you, Tane."

"So formal." Tane half turned towards me and I couldn't help but mirror him, my heart pounding. "We're friends, right?"

I nodded. "Yeah."

"I don't really know what I'm going to do." Tane's voice turned a little more serious. "I don't know... I've run away from my whole career and every time I think about going back to it, it's like I shut down. It scares me so bad. But I really, really like hanging out with you, Dillon."

"Do you have to go back?" Suddenly I was imagining Tane moved in, cooking some nights, coming home from the shop to find him here, settled in, his books shelved with mine... married? A happy, boring couple who lived in a small town and ran a store together? Could he ever be happy with that?

Tane smacked his lips and leaned back against the couch. "I have a contract, at least one more album with this company, and my manager will raise Hell if I bail on that, I'd have to pay out a lot of money if I don't deliver... but... really those are my only commitments? I have an apartment back in L.A. but I could get rid of that easily enough." He sighed, meeting my eyes with intensity.

I sensed the pull of something from him. He needed something very badly. What was it? Stability? Comfort? A loving husband? I could give him those things — although I was clearly getting very ahead of myself with the husband thing. But there was a spark between us, I was sure of that.

"Tane, I really like you. I know we hardly know each other, but—"

"But it's like we've known each other for years, somehow." Tane took my hand, a tentative gesture. I squeezed his fingers, rubbing the calluses on his fingers. "I like you too, Dillon. I can't stop thinking about you and what—" he swallowed his next words but I thought I could guess them.

"What would it be like to try?" I whispered.

Tane nodded.

Chapter Eight

Dillon

I didn't overthink it. I leaned in and kissed those beautiful lips.

He put his arm around my waist and pulled me closer and I moaned into his mouth. His lips were pillowy soft, and his tongue quick when I opened my mouth to it.

All we were doing was kissing but it felt like the single most romantic, and erotic moment of my life. Everything in me was shouting "Yes! More please!" so I went ahead and murmured that into the miss.

Tane chuckled and pulled me fully onto his lap. I settled there like I was born to it, my knees squeezing against his hips. I cupped his cheek with one hand and kissed him deep.

My blood roared in my veins, wanting more and more. He bucked his hips up and I felt his hardness through his jeans and groaned.

Before we went any further we had to talk about some guidelines though…

With extreme reluctance, I pulled back. "Uh, so I really like you and that was awesome, but I uh, well we should talk."

"Talk about what?" Tane smirked, and rubbed his hand up and down my thigh. It was highly distracting.

"No uh, full sex on the first date, especially after a meal like that one," I said, blushing hard but not caring. Sex stuff was important to me and we had to talk it out so there wasn't confusion.

"Okay, fair enough," Tane said. "How do you feel about hand stuff on the first date? Although we could argue this is the second..."

I ignored his second statement and took a deep breath. I was hard against my pants and it was beginning to be a problem. "Hands and mouths are all good."

Tane grinned wide. "Really?"

"Yes, and I don't know if you're a top or a bottom or a side, or whatever?"

Tane shrugged one shoulder. "I'm easy, I'll do whatever, I like it all ways."

I grinned, blushing even harder. "Okay. I like to bottom most of the time but sometimes I want to switch."

"Perfect. You're perfect." Tane pulled me down for another kiss and I groaned into it.

"Maybe we should move to the bedroom?"

Tane stood up, one hand slipping under my ass and the other tight around my waist, lifting me like I weighed nothing. I flushed all over again.

"That's... very hot."

"Thank you. Which one's your room?"

I twisted to point it out, wrapping my legs around his waist and thrilling at the warmth of him, how much I wanted to see him naked, to feel him pinning me down.

But I'd also basically asked to go slow. Not entirely slow, but... slow-ish. He'd said he couldn't stop thinking about me and now he was carrying me to bed. I was almost dizzy with excitement.

I flicked the light on as he carried me into my own bedroom. It was tidy, thankfully I'm anal enough about tidiness that I didn't need to panic about an unexpected guest, but I hoped he didn't judge the room for its blandness.

Tane sat on the bed and kissed me again.

I moved my hands to undo the buttons of his shirt, I needed to touch his skin. Needed to feel him.

He helped me to remove his shirt, and then went to work on mine.

He had a spattering of tattoos over his chest, the warm brown of his skin offset by blue-black ink depicting stars in a constellation I didn't recognise. I ran my fingers over them. "This is pretty."

"It's the southern cross," he said. "It's a constellation you only see from the Southern Hemisphere. My stage name, Whetu, means star, so I got this tattoo when I first charted, in honour of home."

I leaned in and kissed the stars, making him giggle.

"I'd like to see it someday." Dillon straightened up to kiss Tane's jaw, enjoying the graze of the stubble against his lips. "I guess I never thought about there being different stars."

"It's a trip." Tane's hands trailed slowly over Dillon's chest, then down to grip his waist, pulling him closer. "Not seeing it at night, can feel kind of lonely."

"I can imagine." Dillon pushed gently at Tane's shoulders, encouraging him to lay back. He did so, his hands trailing over me, refusing to let go entirely. I shuffled back to undo his jeans, one hand stroking him through the denim. He was hard, and large.

It had been some time since I had hooked up with anyone, but some things you don't forget how to do. I leaned in to kiss and lick at his nipples. I slipped my hand inside his jeans to grip his hardness in my hand, stroking as much as I could in the confined space.

He moaned, a deliciously deep sound that resonated in his chest.

Tane's hand moved up to stroke my hair, fingers carding through and then gently pushing my head further down. I chuckled, getting the hint.

Shoving his jeans down but leaving his boxer briefs in place, I mouthed over the end of him. He smelled like hot sweat and I wanted to lick him all over. But we were going slow. Slow.

I teased him a while longer, licking until his underwear was wet and he was panting hard.

"Tease..." he growled.

His fingers tightened in my hair and pulled. I let myself be moved, more turned on than I'd ever been, that I could remember.

One hand in my hair and the other on my hip, he flipped us so I landed on my back with a grunt. He let go long enough to strip me of my pants and underwear.

"You're so hard, baby..." Tane said, taking me in.

Exposed, I wanted to hide my face, but I didn't want to stop looking at him. My cheeks were on fire, and I regretted telling him no full sex. Looking at this man in front of me with a little pot belly and strong arms, I wanted to feel every bit of him.

But this was enough, enough for tonight at least.

"Want you so bad," I murmured, hardly audible.

"Yeah?" He stroked me with one hand and leaned in to lick over the tip of me, his tongue teasing at my foreskin and making me writhe. "God you're beautiful, Dillon. Want to tie you down and tease you for hours, see you really come apart.

I slapped one of my hands over my eyes. His words set fire through me and I could feel myself pulsing under his ministrations.

"Please, it's been ... I can't hold back," I gasped.

"Don't hold back." Tane chuckled, that low, warm sound and wrapped his full lips around me, bobbing his head down.

I bucked my hips and he slipped his hand down to tease at my taint, pressing and stroking in just the right places until I was coming into his mouth.

I whimpered, embarrassed at how quickly I'd come, like a teenager with a crush. But Tane licked me clean, slow and affectionate and then he took me in his arms and kissed me hard. I tasted a trace of salt on his tongue, it sent me into overdrive.

Slipping my hand between us, I wrapped my hand around him and pumped. He was throbbing almost instantly, and I was overwhelmed with how pleased I was, that he was as into me as I was into him.

He broke the kiss to gasp for air and I nipped his jaw and mouthed up to his earlobe. He came quietly, the softest moan and a jerk of the hips before the heat of his come hit my hand.

"So gorgeous," I breathed.

"You're so good." He pulled me tight against his chest and I relaxed there, gently stroking him until he was all spent. Content as a kitten, practically purring, I nuzzled under his chin.

After a moment more, I let go and he eased his grip, I grabbed some tissues to clean him up.

"That was..." I tried to describe how perfect it had been, how much I wanted more, how much I wanted him. The words didn't come.

"Everything." He said. "That was everything."

I tossed the tissues in the bin and grabbed a water bottle, swigging from it before offering it to Tane. "Yes, it was."

"Thanks." He downed the rest of the water. "Need anything else?"

I traced the tattoos on his chest with one finger. He shook his head. "I can get going if you want?"

"No." My fingers tightened, as if I could grip his shoulder and hold him in place. "I mean, uh. Please stay?"

Tane nodded. "I'd love to."

"I even have pjs you can borrow, if you want?"

"I usually sleep naked," he said. I almost swooned.

"Okay. I'm going to brush my teeth, I have a spare toothbrush you can use."

"Perfect, you're perfect."

Tane

I wasn't usually much of a cuddler. I wasn't much of a relationship guy, really. I'd dated men, women, a non-binary person, but... dated probably wasn't even the right word. These were one-night stands, or party hookups that I'd see once every few months and fuck, and then we'd be done until the next industry gig.

I'd never had anyone I wanted to stay overnight with and snuggle.

What was Dillon doing to me?

I slept so well, wrapped in Dillon's strong farm-boy arms. (I knew he wasn't a farm boy, not by a long shot, but I can have my fantasies), and his soft bedding, his patchwork quilt clearly made by a loving family member and I was safe. Safe, content and more than anything, like I'd come home.

When I woke in the early morning light, Dillon stirred as well, yawning softly. He hummed when I met his eyes, his own crinkling with pleasure.

"Good morning."

"Morning."

"Want me to make you breakfast?"

I shook my head. "I'm not a breakfast person, thanks though."

"Ah well, some other time." Dillon tensed the moment after he'd said it, as if he'd realised the implication.

"Next time." I said it firmly, and sealed it with a kiss of promise. I didn't know for sure what the future held, but more and more I wanted it to hold Dillon. I wanted this. This room, this bed, this man. I wanted to feel safe and at home. I'd never felt that way in L.A. In fact, anywhere in the United States until now, and I hadn't even realised I was missing that security. Not until I was shown it, with gentle kindness by a sweet and straightforward man.

Dillon sat up slowly, so I sat up too. "You're missing out, breakfast isn't just the most important meal of the day, it's often the most delicious."

I chuckled, sitting up, swinging my legs off the bed so I could hide a little of the bliss I was feeling. I didn't want him to see the future I was planning in my head and freak out. I had too many things to sort out — I wondered if my manager would ship my clothes and things from L.A.? Or if he'd take me to court...

We got ready together in companionable silence. Dillon went out of his way to touch me or give me a little kiss on the cheek as we passed. It was sweet, and comfortable, and almost dangerous in how addictive it could become. Could I allow myself to have something like this?

I walked Dillon to the grocery shop, and when we got there he slipped his arm around me and gave me the kind of kiss that made me weak in the knees. I pulled back with a reluctant hum. "You need to open up the place."

"I'm the owner, I can be a couple of minutes late. How about I walk you back to the motel?"

I giggled, a kid again, and nodded. "Yeah, sure."

He held my hand as we walked. I looked around, unsure if this little town would be welcoming to open displays of affection between two men, but no one gave us a second glance. I was walking on air, high, jubilant. I bit my lip, because I felt something else, too.

Something familiar, but that I hadn't felt in a very long time.

I was inspired. Like I could write a song about this.

How very cliché of me. One fun-filled night with a handsome man and I was back in the writing game?

I shook my head, laughing at myself.

"What is it?" Dillon asked.

I looked at him sideways, the gentle crease of his forehead and knew without a doubt I could love this man. I could spend the rest of my days with him, make a happy life, write new songs… and I wasn't even afraid?

We reached the edge of town and my little U-shaped motel. It didn't even look sad in the morning light, it looked like an important milestone on my road to happiness. *Cliché, cliché, cliché* but whatever, clichés exist for a reason, sometimes they explain something universal, right?

Well, that's what I told myself.

We were crossing the parking lot when the door in the tiny reception office banged open. I turned to look at the noise just as an all-too-familiar voice shouted my name.

"Tane! There you are! Where have you been all night?"

Andrew Lane stomped across the asphalt towards me like a horror movie villain.

I let go of Dillon's hand. "Andrew, why are you here?"

He was livid, his cheeks red, and he'd obviously slept in his designer casual suit.

"Since you haven't bothered to turn on your phone in days, I've been reduced to scouring the gossip columns and social media. Someone thought they saw you in this God-forsaken town, so I drove down here. Turns out it was true. You've been hiding here, then?" Andrew gave Dillon the scornful up-and-down look that I was used to seeing from him before a public appearance. "With this?"

"I..." I shook my head. "Andrew, listen, I just needed a break."

"What about your commitments? What about your tour schedule? What about the album?" Andrew was practically spitting. The guy who ran the desk during the day at the motel was watching from the doorway. Thankfully he wasn't filming on his phone, but surely it was a matter of time. Someone walking his dog had stopped on the road, and was holding his phone up. We had to get out of the public eye.

"You can't talk to him like that." Dillon had puffed himself up, was standing taller, and his chest and shoulders looked huge.

Andrew narrowed his eyes. "Who do you think you are? Some hayseed from nowhere? You slept with him did you? Good for you, now leave us alone."

I could see how this would go. Good, honest Dillon versus my asshole Hollywood agent? I had to get Dillon out of there.

"Dillon, thanks, but I think you should go. I can handle this."

Dillon frowned. "But he's treating you like garbage."

I sighed. "Yeah, he does sometimes, but I know what I'm doing. He's right, I do have commitments, I'll call you later, okay?"

I could see how much Dillon didn't want to go. He leaned in and kissed my cheek. "Call if you need me," he murmured.

"I will."

Dillon gave Andrew the stink eye and then stalked off.

"What am I going to do with you?" Andrew said.

I sighed. "What am I going to do? That's the big question."

"First of all we'll get you out of this dump." Andrew gestured at the motel. "Straight back to Los Angeles."

"No." I folded my arms. "I'm staying in Foggy Basin while we figure this out."

Andrew rolled his eyes. "Well, I'm not staying in this motor inn, I'll find us a Bed and Breakfast or something more palatable."

"Fine." I looked back towards where Dillon had walked and pulled out my room key. "I'll pack up my stuff."

Chapter Nine

Dillon

I was distracted all morning.

No wonder why. I was torn between the joyful memories of the night before and the frankly shocking encounter with Tane's manager first thing. I couldn't stop thinking about the sneer on the man's face, the way he'd looked at Tane like he was nothing. Not a person, but a meal ticket, a money-earner and nothing more.

It was revolting, that someone could look at another human that way. It was especially horrible that it was Tane. Tane, who was sweet, and a little shy despite all his fame and success. Tane who made delicious bread and had bonded with my little sister.

"You want me to take over at the till?" Christian asked after I'd been there an hour, brooding and glaring out the window.

"I'm fine," I snapped at him. I instantly regretted it. Christian was being sweet and trying to help. "Sorry, yes, that'd be great. I'll go... look at the takings or something."

I retreated to the backroom and fussed with the things on my desk. They all seemed to be out of place, somehow. I tidied what I could.

It wasn't enough. I still felt out-of-sorts and angry.

Well, I knew why. I fired off a quick text to Tane asking how he was doing.

I made myself a cup of coffee. Then brought up my financial spreadsheets and sales reports.

Things weren't going well.

I frowned at the spreadsheet. I hadn't noticed a particular drop off in customers, but it appeared people weren't buying as much as they used to? I wondered if there was something at work I didn't know about. Did we need to sign up to Instacart or something like that? Who'd do the deliveries?

But maybe people were ordering stuff in from the next town?

Why would they do that?

Did they miss my parents that much?

I glanced at the pinboard where Mom and Dad's latest postcard looked back at me, judging.

There was something wrong. Had I made too much of a change by ordering in new kinds of food?

I couldn't work it out.

Around midday, Ivy came into the backroom. Her face was uncharacteristically blank.

"Dill, I need to talk to you." Her voice was tense, and when I searched her eyes I could see something serious had happened. I pushed my chair back from the desk and looked up at her.

"Yeah? Here or do you want to go grab a coffee?"

"Here's fine." Ivy grabbed the spare stool and straddled it. She took a deep breath. "Dillon, I need to tell you something."

I bit my lip, suddenly worried. Our parents were away and Ivy had come to me with something deadly serious. Was she pregnant? What would I do? I barely contained myself from blurting out 'I'll look after your baby!', I didn't want to jump to conclusions.

"Uh huh," I said instead.

Ivy hesitated further and I realised I could be more supportive of whatever she was going through. "I'm here for you, baby sister."

Ivy took a heavy, loaded breath. "That's... well, that's just it. Dillon, I..."

She hesitated. I bit my lip. I didn't want to force her to say anything she wasn't ready to say. But I didn't want to butt in either. I nodded, trying to encourage her.

"I don't think I'm your sister."

I blinked. What could she mean? Were our parents not our parents? Was she adopted? No, there was no chance. I remember Mom being pregnant with her.

"What... what do you mean?"

"Dill, I think I'm trans. I've been feeling a sort of way lately, and things are grating on me, and I think... I think I'm your baby *brother.*"

Relief flooded me. No baby to worry about.

Ivy, however, needed my full support right then. I took both of her... no, his hands in mine. His pronouns were he/him now. I adjusted my thinking.

"Okay. You're my baby brother. Do you have a new name I should call you?"

Ivy blinked at me. Then swallowed. "That's it? That's all you have to say?"

"Uh, yeah?" I shuffled my chair closer to him. "I love you, you're my sibling, and that won't change even if you do. I mean, you didn't freak out when I told you I was gay, did you?"

Ivy teared up, his face contorting into a picture of misery. He threw his arms around me and sobbed. "You're the best brother ever!"

I hugged him tight, smiling a little to myself. I was pretty sure I'd nailed that conversation. Ivy was crying but surely it was from relief. Coming out, as I knew, was always a vulnerable experience. It was impossible to predict how someone would react to your announcement, and any kind of rejection could be devastating, especially from a family member.

After a while Ivy pulled away, yanking a tissue out from his pocket to mop at his face. "Fuck. That was scary.""Yeah, I bet." I grabbed my water bottle and handed it to him. "Drink."

"Thanks." Ivy took a deep swig and then smacked his lips. "You're so cool."

I smiled at him. "How about I take the afternoon off, leave Christian in charge and take you to Hartsville?"

Ivy blinked. "Hartsville?"

"Yeah it's the closest department store. We can get you new clothes and pajamas and stuff."

Ivy teared up again, bent forward and buried his face in his hands.

I patted his back, got up and went to check that Christian was okay with sole charge. "Bit of a family emergency, nothing bad, just... Ivy needs me."

Christian nodded and smiled his easy-going smile. "No worries. I'll lock up with the spare key, take care."

I drove the thirty miles to Hartsville, the biggest closest town, and Ivy told me about his journey — feeling not quite right about his gender, researching online and talking with some friends who had already transitioned at the university.

He didn't need me to say much, just affirm him and say I understood, and I could tell he needed to off-load all of this. Neither of us brought up our parents. I sensed it was a bit too soon for that.

I parked at Target and we went inside, grabbing a cart. I led him straight to the Menswear section.

"How do we start?"

"Start with the basics. Underwear first, then pants, then shirts." I nodded, confident. "It just makes sense."

"I'm glad I have you, Dill. I don't think I'd be brave enough to do this on my own." He glanced around and I shook my head.

"Trust me, no one cares what you buy. And this is a good, cheap way to work out what kind of style you want. Uh, by the way, you never told me if you have a new name?"

"Name's are hard," Ivy said. "I'm toying with a few options, I want to keep the plant theme... maybe Briar, or Aster?"

"Those are both excellent options. Just take your time, you don't want to pick something that doesn't sit right."

Ivy nodded and I led him to the men's underwear section. "Go ahead, pick whatever."

Ivy bit his lip and started sorting through boxer briefs. "How do I know my size?"

"I'd guess you're a small."

Ivy started loading things into the cart. I added a pack of simple white T-shirts for myself in large, Ivy noticed, and grabbed the same pack but in small. My heart thumped.

"Onto jeans, I have no idea of sizing there, so you'll need to try on some other options."

I checked on my phone a couple of times, but Tane never replied. Thinking about Tane, or the sales at the shop was too much. When I tried to, my brain just clouded over with static.

Whatever. I have a little brother now.

I focussed on Ivy. Ivy needed me. I could be there for Ivy.

Chapter Nine

Tane

A ndrew had found a little short term rental a few miles out of town. We sat down and discussed terms.

Well, more accurately, we fought.

He wanted me to fulfil my contract, release the next album, and probably one more. I had concerts booked, he wanted me to do those. He wanted me to wait to make any kind of decision. He wanted me to come back to L.A.

But the more I thought about any of that stuff, the more I wanted to just quit it all.

"You should never give up on your dreams, though." Andrew shook his head like I was talking nonsense.

I sat back, considering. I'd grown up on messages like that too.

"Okay, but what if the dream isn't what I thought it'd be?"

"What's bugging you? Can we make it easier? You want more time between concerts, we can make that happen — it'll cost us more but we'll work something out. Maybe you could do more low-key appearances, smaller venues?"

After a few hours of this, my head was pounding. I was on the verge of a realisation, so I excused myself to go outside and breathe the fresh air. Country air.

L.A. was anathema to me, now. The smell of the smog, the heat, the people with their fake tans and filler in their cheeks and protein shakes and telling you they love you when it's all just a facade to get themselves ahead?

I needed something real, at least for a while. If I was going to make music again it wouldn't be the same as it was before. It would come from my heart. Maybe it would be outside my usual genre, and that's fine. Maybe it was time for Whetu to retire, so I could just be Tane.

And I knew exactly who I wanted to be Tane with, and where.

I went back inside.

"How much would I have to pay, if I canceled my contract?"

Andrew's mouth disappeared into a thin line of anger. "Don't be hasty, now."

"I'm not being hasty." I shook my head. "I want out. I know I'll be disappointing fans, I'll post on socials and explain myself. But I can't do it again. I don't have another Whetu album in me. I'm retiring."

"Tane, please—"

I picked up my jacket and my keys, pleased I'd driven us there in my rental so I could leave again. "I'm out, Andrew. I'll get in touch with my lawyer,

I'll pay out what I owe, but please don't make this more difficult. I'll go to court if I have to."

I went out to the car, Andrew climbed in on the passenger side. "Tane, no, listen to me, you have to reconsider."

He tried to talk me out of it all the way back to Foggy Basin. I turned the music up.

It was getting close to six by the time we rolled back into town. It had been a long day and I was worn out, but also kind of exhilarated. I knew what I wanted, I knew what I wanted my future to be.

I pulled up outside Foggy Basin Grocer's to see Christian locking the door.

I wound down the window. "Hey, Christian, is Dillon around?"

Christian squinted at me and shook his head. "Nah, he had a family emergency, he's been gone all afternoon with Ivy."

My stomach swooped. Was Ivy okay? Had something happened with their parents?

I went to check my phone and saw a few missed messages from Dillon. He was asking if I was okay.

My shoulders released some tension.

I called him.

"Hello, Tane?" He answered on the third ring. "You okay?"

"Yeah, I'm okay. Are you?"

"Yeah." Someone said something in the background and Dillon said faintly. "He's okay. I'm just chilling out with my brother."

"Your brother?"

"Yeah, Ivy came out to me. We're brainstorming names. You should join us."

"I'd love to. You got dinner? I could pick up some tacos from that place, Garcias?"

"Perfect. See you soon."

I drove to the motel and parked up.

Andrew was making disbelieving scoffing noises. "You're just going to have tacos with that guy?"

"Yes, Andrew. And you should head back to L.A." I got out and went to the taco truck, ordering up way more burritos and tacos than the three of us would need. Andrew followed me.

"Tane, I'm not just giving up on you, on this, you have a massive talent and I won't let you just throw it all away."

The taco truck guy gave him a disbelieving look. I shook my head and put my hand on his shoulder.

"Andrew. I'm letting you go, I'm quitting music, I'm done. There's nothing more to it. I'll call my lawyer first thing in the morning."

Andrew pulled away from my hand and swore. He pulled out his phone and made some calls.

Dillon drove up in a beat up old station wagon. He grinned wide at me. "Thought you might want some help carrying everything."

I hugged him tight, more grateful than I would have guessed to see him. To feel how sturdy he felt in my arms.

Dillon hugged me back just as hard and I thought I could feel him trembling a little.

When we finally let go he nodded at Andrew. "What's going on?"

"I've told him to get lost," I said. "I'm quitting music, for the moment anyway."

Dillon's eyes widened. "You are?"

"Yeah. It's time to face facts. I'm burned out, plain and simple. I need down time."

"Good for you."

We both regarded Andrew, who was spitting curses into the phone, and looking more and more angry. Finally he slammed his phone into his pocket and came over, stomping his feet like a child having a tantrum.

"Your contract is iron-clad, Tane. You're coming back with me and you're finishing that album."

I rolled my eyes. "Don't be stupid, you can't force me to do anything."

"I can and I will. I'll do that thing, what happened to Britney? You're obviously not stable and can't be trusted to make your own decisions. Get in the car. You owe me that album, I'm relying on the royalties from it."

He went to grab my arm.

I was gaping, disbelieving what he'd said. He couldn't mean that, it was absolutely ludicrous.

Dillon intercepted, putting himself between Andrew and me. "Back off, Hollywood."

Andrew spat on the ground. "Who the hell do you think you are, farm boy? Tane's a star, and I made him that way. You have no idea what you're getting into with him. Don't piss me off, or I'll..."

Dillon squared up, suddenly all broad shoulders and buff chest. His voice dropped low. "Or you'll what?"

Andrew took a step back. "Whatever. You better have a good lawyer, because I'm going to do everything I can to screw you over, Tane!"

"Just go, Andrew. You're fired. I'm contesting the contract, and you'll hear from my lawyer first thing in the morning." I was heartsick and tired. This was all so over-dramatic. So deeply *stupid*. I wanted him gone and I never wanted to see him again.

Andrew looked Dillon over.

Dillon took a step forward and Andrew backed up to his rental car. "You'll regret this!"

"I already regret ever hiring you." I turned my back on him and rolled my eyes at the taco truck guy.

Andrew's rental took off with a wheel spin and way too much acceleration. I could hear him shouting something out the window but I couldn't make it out.

Something loosened in my chest. Andrew Lane driving away felt like the end of the chapter. Well, I knew I'd still have to deal with him, so not exactly the end. The start of the end, maybe. There might be a song in that.

Making him give up on me had been difficult and now that it was done I was pleased, but a little disappointed as well. It had only taken a few hours really, to get him to give up. Wasn't I worth fighting for, a little longer at least?

It was for the best, and he'd been an asshole, but something inside still hurt. I wished he'd been a better person, maybe.

Dillon watched him go then slipped an arm around my shoulders. "That guy's a piece of work."

I leaned into him, borrowing some of his surety and his strength.

"Yeah. I mean, I kinda knew that but a lot of agents, they tell you what they want to hear. You don't get to see the asshole until it's too late." I leaned into Dillon. "Thank you. For standing up for me."

"No one should ever treat you that way. You deserve something better."

I kissed him lightly, more of a thanks than anything else. "Thank you. I think I understand that now."

He gave me a bear hug and I relaxed against him, smelling his scent, woody mixed with fresh flowers.

"I want to stay with you, if that's okay?" I mumbled.

Dillon squeezed me. "I'd like nothing more than that."

We kissed again, slow and dreamy, relaxing into each other.

"Order up!" The taco truck guy broke the spell and we laughed, pulling apart.

We collected the food and Dillon drove us back to his place, all of three minutes in the car.

"So Ivy's okay?" I asked, before we got out of the car.

"Yeah. I guess he was really worried about how I'd take it, how our parents will, but we had a really good afternoon. He bought so many flannel shirts, you won't believe." Dillon laughed. "I love him so much."

We went upstairs together.

Dillon

Over the next few days Tane was distracted, calling his lawyer and dealing with his contract negotiations. I went to work and left him to it, and when I came home at the end of the day he'd be trying to prepare something for dinner.

Ivy chose the name Aster, so Tane and I used it for him as much as possible.

Aster and Tane got on like a house on fire, which was a relief. Since the day we'd gone shopping, Aster had been going out in men's clothes, and had hacked off all his hair. He was shy, but looked great.

Back at the shop the sales were still confounding me. The Korean ingredients I'd ordered weren't moving. It was like everyone in town was afraid of them or something.

I'd tried calling my folks but they seemed to be out of service range.

When I tried to work out what to do, I came up with a blank. My mind just glassed over with nothingness.

Then there was Tane. He'd moved all his stuff in from the motel, it was just ridiculous to be paying for it when he could stay with me for free, after all. But he was so busy with everything going on in his career I didn't know where he and I stood.

He'd been sleeping in my bed, but we'd barely done more than hold hands. He passed out so quickly at night, and I didn't want to bother him further with questions like 'what are we?'

I was afraid I'd scare him off.

I got home at the end of an average Friday and flopped down on the couch.

"What's up, bro?" Aster glanced over at me. He was playing some weird botany game on the Switch.

"I'm struggling."

Tane came into the lounge and crashed down beside me, his knee bumping mine. "Struggling how?"

"The shop." I pressed the palms of my hands onto my eyes, trying to blot out the world. The static in my head was growing, drowning out words, drowning out what I needed to communicate. I could feel my hands were shaking. I was on the verge of some kind of outburst. I had no idea if it was going to be crying or screaming, but something was welling up in me.

The room went silent. The couch cushions shifted.

"Is it okay if I touch you, right now?" Tane's voice was low, careful. Like he was afraid of spooking me. I appreciated it.

I nodded, but I wasn't really sure. Sometimes when I got like this I needed to be alone, with no one touching me.

Gently, he splayed his big hand over my back and pressed gently, rubbing small circles with his fingertips.

Aster moved about the room. I could hear his footsteps, and the sound of his game turned all the way down, then off.

I swallowed, trying to remember how to ground myself.

Tane's fingers. I could feel those. Pressing the soles of my feet into the floor, I concentrated on that gentle pressure.

Then breathing. Slow in and out, in and out.

Tane started to sing, something low, and gentle and beautiful. Another song in Māori, as I didn't understand the words. But it stirred something warm inside of me. Something that chased away a little of the static, and gave me something to hold onto.

A few breaths later, I was able to straighten up and drop my hands from my face. The overwhelm wasn't entirely gone, I'd need to sleep and take some time in silence to really get rid of it, but for the moment, I could cope.

"Welcome back." I looked at Tane, half-expecting to see judgement there, even though he'd been nothing but sweet to me. Instead he was smiling, warm and relieved.

"Thanks. I like the song."

Tane smiled. "It's another one everyone knows back home, a love song."

"Ew, right in front of my salad?" Aster said.

I glanced at him but he didn't have any food in front of him. "Huh?"

"It's an internet meme, don't worry about it."

"Okay." I took another breath. "So the shop, I don't know, I ordered some new Korean foods... the take and bake pizzas are doing well, everything in the chiller is okay, but overall sales are down and I don't know what to do about it."

"No wonder you're stressed out." Tane slipped his arm around me and I leaned back into him.

"Let's brainstorm something. Maybe a big event?" Aster caught Tane's eye. "Maybe with a celebrity guest to draw people's interest?"

Tane smacked his lips.

"You don't have to," I said, quickly. "I know you're in a strange place with music and you're burned out. No, we'll think of something else."

Tane hummed. "I could be into it. Just for an hour or two, play whatever I like, acoustic..." He nodded. "You can count on me."

Aster grinned and hopped up. "I'll get to work on flyers, how long do you need to prepare?"

"I..." I shook my head. "I don't know? What would we do?"

"You could do free samples of the Korean stuff? Maybe bring in some other new, interesting foods?" Tane suggested.

I imagined myself cooking up kimbap and fried chicken, and felt my shoulders relax. "That would be really fun."

"I can do some shifts at the shop if you need cover," Aster said. "But I want to be in charge of marketing for this event, okay? I'm sure we can get traction on social media."

"I can help out with shifts too," Tane said. "There's not much prep I need, just a microphone and a place to stand, really."

I looked between them, hardly daring to believe... but they were both utterly sincere and looking back at me with excitement.

"Okay, um, yes. Let's book this in, how about two weeks on Saturday?"

"Perfect!" Aster dashed out of the room.

Tane stroked my hair back from my face and looked deep into my eyes. "What else do you need, Dill?"

I took another breath and shook my head. "I just need to be in quiet a while longer, if that's okay?"

"No worries, I'll get us something for dinner. You sit here and take all the time you need."

He kissed my forehead — an act that had butterflies hatching through my stomach and went into the kitchen. Aster must have dialed the lights down in the living room because nothing was too bright.

I hugged a cushion to my chest and lay down on my side, letting my brain accept that I was okay, there was nothing to be afraid of, and I had two wonderful people who were going to help with the shop.

Chapter Ten

Dillon

The two weeks before the event passed in a pleasant blur. I blew my own budget, ordering in food for the big day, and practicing how to cook it all.

True to their words, Aster and Tane came through, covering the till in the shop, and I got Christian in for some more shifts as well.

Aster had launched the store on all forms of social media he could find, and had already amassed quite a following. Although, when it came to listing the attractions of the day, Tane hadn't been announced. He was billed as '*mystery celebrity guest*' and the comments on all the posts were going wild trying to guess who it could be.

Finally, the big day arrived. I was relieved when it dawned sunny and clear.

We'd decorated with fairy lights and bright streamers in every colour of the rainbow.

Aster had hired a popcorn cart from somewhere and manned it out the front with a striped apron over his jeans and button-down shirt.

I'd pre-prepared as much food as I could, and there were stations around the store where people could pick up samples.

I went to start up the cotton candy machine, the last thing I had to do before opening, and was surprised to find a queue of people waiting to come in.

Aster was already handing out little boxes of popcorn to the crowd.

I hurriedly flipped the sign and threw the door open. "Welcome in, everyone!"

The next few hours passed in a blur. Handing out samples, talking to everyone I could manage. Many regulars complimented me on the new stock, and on how nice the shop looked. None of them said anything about not being in so often, but I wasn't about to confront anyone when the day was going so well.

At midday, Tane came out to stand in front of the shop. I'd organised him a microphone, and offered to introduce him but he turned me down. "I've got this, Dill."

I stepped out to watch, dusting my hands off on my apron.

Tane stepped up to the mic, guitar in hand and surveyed the crowd. For a moment he looked uncertain, and my heart thudded. This was worlds away from the stadiums I'd seen footage of him performing in, it was nothing like a crowd of devoted fans, but it must surely be frightening all the same.

Tane

My stomach twisted. I knew these people were locals, they were here to celebrate Dillon and his shop, and not here to see me because ... well, they'd had no real idea I'd be there performing. I'd gotten to know some faces from putting on the Foggy Basin Grocer's apron and working the till but I didn't think many knew my stage name.

I wanted to play. I wanted to make this something wonderful. I wanted, more than anything, to break the block I'd had around performing.

I scanned the crowd, aware I was taking too long to say anything.

I cleared my throat.

"Gidday everyone, my name's Tane." There was a smattering of applause.

"Yeah, Tane!" Aster called from the popcorn cart.

I strummed my guitar, then faltered, uncertain, what was I going to sing? I'd made myself a mental playlist but I couldn't remember any of it now.

Sweat beaded on my forehead as the silence stretched out. How did I used to do this? It was terrifying. Absolutely terrifying.

How had I managed all those nights? All those concerts? Had I just been getting drunk before each show? Maybe. There had definitely been some pharmaceutical assistance at times.

Or was there some skill I'd lost? The knack of going out on stage, confident that people wanted to see me, and that I had talent.

I'd lost that knowledge somewhere along the way.

But people were here to be entertained. They hadn't necessarily come for me, but to see something. I could be that something, couldn't I?

I caught sight of Dillon. He was smiling at me, confident and proud. He gave me a thumbs up.

Dillon believed in me.

I breathed out. I was going to start with *Slice of Heaven* by The Herbs and Dave Dobbyn, that was it. A chill, catchy Kiwi song that hopefully, people would sing along with once they caught the chorus.

Strumming the old, familiar tune, I started to sing.

Time slipped away on me and I lost myself in the music. This felt easy. Singing, playing my guitar, and smiling at the crowd who were swaying and clapping in time.

Some of them did learn the chorus and sung along on the second time around. It was a good vibe.

This was why I did it. I'd lost track of it somewhere, somehow along the way, but now it came back to me. This ancient art of music making, of simply raising my voice in song, I felt connected to my ancestors, and to every troubadour and song-writer who'd ever come before me.

I was part of a greater whole. The human need to create, to share, to sing and to dance, for a moment I was a conduit of that once more.

Moving into my second and third songs, some of the New Zealand songs that I knew had charted overseas, and after a couple of Māori waiata, I performed the first song I'd ever got a number one charted position for. *Take Me Home* had come from a place of homesickness, and feeling like I didn't belong, but the song changed during the verses, and became a song of love and hope.

This was what I wanted.

I wanted to make music that made people happy. I didn't want to make music to make money for someone else, and I didn't care any more about the charts. I wanted to use my talent to connect.

I finished up the song and was deafened by the force of the applause.

Aster ran up and hugged me tight. He'd got a new binder the day before and he was looking great. I laughed and hugged him with one arm, holding my guitar out of the way.

Dillon gently took the guitar off me and set it aside before hugging me too.

"Your voice is so beautiful Tane, it was like being transported or something."

Dillon and I hadn't really spoken about our relationship. We'd slept in the same bed for two weeks but the most we did was peck each other on the cheek or hold hands.

Now that I'd had my epiphany about what I wanted from my music, I knew what I wanted from Dillon too.

Aster moved back and I cupped Dillon's chin in one hand. "Hey Dill?"

"Yeah?"

"Want to be my boyfriend?"

Dillon beamed so hard his eyes crinkled closed. "Yes! Hell, I want to be your husband, Tane."

I laughed and tugged him in for a kiss. "One step at a time, but... yes. I want that too."

Dillon rubbed his stubbled cheek against mine and pressed his forehead against me. "You make me so happy, Tane."

I kissed him deeper, tipping him back a little and there was another round of applause.

"It's about time you settled down, Dillon!" Evelyn shouted.

Dillon laughed, wiping tears from his eyes. "Thank you Evelyn!"

I grabbed the microphone. "Now everyone, get on into the store and buy up, there's some great specials and some cool new ingredients you should try!"

Dillon laughed as people began to file inside. Quite a few people came up to tell me how much they'd enjoyed my set, and a few revealed that they knew I was Whetu.

The lanky teen I'd seen busking with the violin approached last. "Hey, um. I guess you're probably really busy and stuff, Mister Tane, but I was wondering if you'd ever consider um, maybe teaching music?"

I blinked at the kid and smiled. "Sure, what's your name?"

"Henry." He held out a hand and I shook it.

"I'd love to tutor you, although from what I've heard of you playing, I don't know how much I can teach, you're very talented. But hey, I'm down."

Henry grinned wide. "Really? That's amazing, I can't afford too much but—"

I held up by hand to stop him. "Nah, don't worry about cash. I can tell you love music, I want to share that with you."

Henry bobbed his head. "Awesome. I'll um, come find you here?"

I nodded. "Maybe I'll put up a notice or something, see if there's any other budding musicians around who might want to jam."

"Right on."

I spent a while longer out the front, chatting to people, and promising that I'd perform again, maybe at the open mic at the bar or something. Then I went in to help bag groceries. I could tell from the number of people checking out, and from the smile on Dillon's face that the event had been a huge success.

My heart swelled with warmth.

I sent up a silent prayer of thanks to whatever had drawn me to this funny little town, and to Dillon. Things weren't entirely resolved with Andrew Lane, but my lawyer was confident we could get a settlement in another week or so, and then I'd truly be free to do whatever I chose.

And I chose this: a grocer for a boyfriend, and someday a husband, a new little brother, a new home, and a new sense of purpose for my music.

I couldn't wait to get my new life started.

Dillon

That night, once Aster had gone to bed, Tane turned to me, his eyes alight with something intriguing.

"What's up?"

"You basically asked me to marry me today." He took my hand in his.

"Well, yeah." My cheeks burned "Like, in the future, though."

He moved closer, cupping my jaw in his hand. "You must really like me."

I laughed, turning my face to kiss his palm. "Isn't it obvious?"

"I dunno." His voice teasing. "We haven't done much more than hold hands aside from that one time..."

I was instantly aroused, my pants getting tight, so I sunk my teeth gently into the meaty part of his palm. I was rewarded with a soft moan "Are you propositioning me, Tane?"

"I am. You into it?"

I nodded and climbed into his lap. "I'm very into it. We should definitely consummate this relationship."

Tane gripped my waist and pulled me closer into him. He was strong, and it shot arousal through my veins.

"Maybe we ought to move to the bedroom?"

"In a moment." Tane pulled me in for a kiss that would have had my knees buckling if I was standing. Instead I squeezed my knees around his hips and rocked my hips. I could feel his hardness under me and it spurred me on to move even more.

"Okay, now we gotta move." Tane stood, lifting me to my feet. I wondered if he'd be able to carry me... now wasn't the time to work that out, not with Aster in the next room.

I led the way to the bedroom, stripping off my shirt and dropping it in the laundry hamper.

Tane's hand on my back was warm and rough, pushing me towards the bed faster so I stumbled a little. "Eager are you?"

"Get naked and on the bed, Dillon, or I swear to God..." his voice had dropped low and the tone of it was full of promise.

Part of me wanted to know exactly what he was threatening me with, but for the moment, I just wanted to feel him inside me. I undid my belt and shoved my jeans down, stepping out of them. I crawled up onto the bed and grabbed out a condom and lube from my sidetable drawer. Turning back, I paused, watching Tane removing his shirt. His skin was a beautiful deep tan colour, and he had a blue-black tattoo forming a cuff around his upper arm. He wasn't as slim as he'd been when he'd first arrived in Foggy Basin, I'd been feeding him regularly, which I think he'd been missing. But he had filled out beautifully.

My mouth watered, and I beckoned for him, unable to wait.

Tane stripped off the rest of his clothes and pushed me down on my back, climbing on top of me to kiss me roughly. I moaned, responding by touching his chest and stroking my fingers down his stomach.

"You're so damn handsome," Tane said.

"I was thinking the same..." I was already panting, so ready for more with this wonderful, kind man.

"Spread your legs for me, pretty."

I did as he asked and he grabbed the lube. He moved fast, squirting the liquid onto his fingers and then smearing it around my hole, massaging with deft precision.

I arched my back, moaning. I slipped one hand between us to stroke him, the other arm hooked around his neck to keep him close.

"Feel good?" He mouthed over my neck, moving his lips up to nip at my earlobe. "Want to make you feel so good, Dillon."

"You do," I said.

He pushed a finger inside and gently worked me open, making me whine with a pathetically audible amount of neediness. "So good. Please, faster."

"Patience, baby, it'll be so good if you let me work my magic."

"Magic fingers." I imagined I could feel the guitar calluses on his fingers, rubbing against the inside of me in the most intimate way possible.

I was sweating, clinging to him with a ferocious need. I hadn't been with anyone in a long time, that was true enough, but it was more than that. The weeks we'd had together, just co-habitating, and getting to know each other, had done nothing but heighten my desire to be with him like this. I was falling in love with him, I knew I was, and this experience was promising only to cement that attraction.

Finally he added some more lube and knelt up above me.

I grabbed the condom, rolling it on for him.

His expression was lustful, but also surprisingly fond as he watched me. "Thank you," he breathed.

Always so polite, even when I was all but begging him to pound me into the mattress.

Once the condom was in place I slicked him with lube and lay back, hitching my knees up. "Please, Tane, I need to feel you. Please?"

He made a noise halfway between a growl and a whine, his eyes going hooded. "Fuck, Dillon..." he pushed inside slowly, letting me stretch and adjust to his thickness. He wrapped one arm around my waist and pulled me closer, until he was entirely inside me, filling me with himself.

I closed my eyes and hid my face against his chest. The stretch was almost painful, but I didn't want him to slow down, I wanted to savour every single second of him.

He kissed my hair and started to thrust. "Is that good?"

"Divine," I breathed, barely audible.

"Good, you're so good for me." He lay us flat on the bed and kissed me deeply, his hips pulsing a gentle thrust, more tease than satisfaction.

He was toying with me, and I loved it.

I wrapped my legs around his hips, encouraging him deeper and faster.

"So good, you feel so good, Tane."

Tane groaned and thrust quicker. "Want to make it last but I'm so hot for you, Dill. I don't think I can—"

I shook my head. "Don't want to wait, just pound me, please!"

His hips moved faster now, and I moaned, letting go of him to throw one of my arms over my eyes and panting.

"You're so handsome, so beautiful, Dill..." he groaned and started pounding me for real. He was panting.

I wanted to look at him.

Moving my arm I regarded him, deep brown eyes and sweat beading on his temples. I wanted to lick it off. I wanted to run my hands through his hair. I wanted to belong to him forever and ever.

His hand closed around my dick and stroked, slick with sweat and lube, my back arched and I cried out. I was moments away from coming and I could feel he was too. His hips stuttered then shoved deep inside me, I came a second later, spilling over his hand.

"God, Dillon..." he breathed.

"I love you, Tane." I reached for him, hardly aware of what I'd said until he wrapped me tight in his arms.

"Aroha nui," he said. "That means, big love. The biggest possible."

I smiled, nuzzling into his neck and inhaling the scent of him. I wanted to commit to memory.

We held each other, still locked together, sweaty and smeared with my seed. We'd need to change the sheets I thought, somewhere in the very back of my mind. But it didn't matter. The rest of me was entirely in the moment, engaged in loving this incredible man who had found his way to my sleepy little town and into my heart.

Epilogue
Tane

Six weeks later

It was Thursday, and the weather was turning a bit colder. Autumn (or fall as the locals would say) was on the way, for sure. I'd spent the morning working at the grocery store, Christian had come down with a cold and I wanted to give Dillon a morning off.

I walked back to the flat humming to myself, my fingers itching to pick up my guitar and play the melody I'd been stuck with all morning.

I had an idea for a song in my head. My muse had been returning to me slowly. And the music it told me to write was entirely different to what I'd been doing before. It was calmer, slower, more folk than hip hop, more soul than club.

I wrote in the mornings, well...most of the time.

Some afternoons and evenings, I tutored Henry. He'd got the word out, I guess, and I'd had some other high school kids, and then some actual adults come to me about teaching them guitar, or singing lessons.

It brought in a little money, but more, it fed my muse. Getting to teach was something I'd never known I wanted to do. It was nice to find a place to slot into the community. Henry said he appreciated how patient I was with him, and I guess the others liked my style as well.

I unlocked the flat door and let myself in, picking up my reliable old guitar and settling on the couch to play the melody. It sounded even better now. I recorded myself playing it, so there was no danger of forgetting.

It had been a couple of weeks since the settlement with Andrew Lane went through — I'd had to pay him and the studio out to cancel my contract, but it was nothing I couldn't bear. I had savings, royalties owed, even.

I looked out the window and my fingers strummed a new phrase for the song. I was coming to love this town.

After the big event at the shop, sales were back where they had been. Dillon speculated that perhaps people were staying away to give him a settling in period, or maybe it had been a seasonal thing?

Whatever the reason, business was buoyant and Dillon wasn't worrying about it any more. In fact he was ordering more Jin ramen and Buldak hot sauce than ever before.

Aster had returned to Sacramento to study, but sent me regular selfies and updates via text. I kept him updated on his brother as well as goings-on in town. (And maybe I sent him a little money for new binders and cool shoes every now and again, but that was between us.)

My phone dinged, drawing my attention to it. It was a relief to not be afraid of my phone anymore.

A selfie. Dillon had got a delivery of BTS branded ramen, and was grinning like a loon in front of it. I sent him back a selfie of myself giving a thumbs up.

I liked the new song, I could make it into something beautiful and upload it.

Every now and then, I'd record a song and upload it to a Soundcloud account I'd started. All acoustic, of course. The music was under my name: Tane, and although I didn't advertise that I was also Whetu, it seemed some of my fans had been looking for me.

I soon had thousands of subscribers for my strange, soft little tunes, and the feedback was overwhelmingly positive. Of course, some of the comments were asking where the club tracks were, but they were by far outnumbered by the fans who connected with my new lyrics, and my new styles. The donations rolled in far faster than I'd expected and there was definitely enough interest for an album.

I rented a small room I could hold music lessons in, and in instruments my students could try out. Next up would be finding a recording studio, but I'd need to go to another town for that.

It could wait.

The next project I had in mind was finding an engagement ring for Dillon.

For some people it might be too soon. I knew my mother would tell me to wait longer. But my soul had recognised something in Dillon, and I knew he felt the same way. It was funny, coming from a place of panic and overwhelm, months ago, to being so sure of my future. I knew what it would be. It would be with Dillon, and a bit of work at the grocer's, tutoring music and releasing a little at a time. Maybe I'd do a concert again, maybe I wouldn't. Someday I'd take Dillon home to Aotearoa so he could see where I'd come from.

For now, I knew Dillon wouldn't be home for hours yet. I set my guitar down and left the flat, hopping in my little secondhand car.

I put on some KPop and drove to Hartsville to check out the jewelers there. I wanted to find him the perfect ring, the perfect symbol of how I felt about him, when I proposed.

I could already imagine his smile, how he'd laugh and kiss me and say something like "yes, of course." I couldn't wait to spend the rest of my life with him.

Life was beautiful, and the best part was?

Even if things got hard, if I got overwhelmed again, or something from my past came back to haunt me? I knew I'd get through it, because I had Dillon, and Dillon had me, and we both had Foggy Basin.

Also by

Jamie Sands

Stay in touch by subscribing to my newsletter

https://greykelpiestudio.eo.page/tk5gx

Mt Eden Witches

Overdues and Occultism

Monsters and Manuscripts

Rituals and Roadtrips

YA novella: Onesies and Ouijaboards

Detective Duarte Mysteries

he Other Side of the Mirror

Reactionary Bewitchment

Monster Slayers (Young adult)

The Suburban Book of the Dead

The Suburban Book of Dreams

Romantic Comedies

Four Years and Today
BEAcon of Love

Under Jaxon Knight
Santa's Sacking
Rival Princes
Mischief and Mayhem
Recipe for Chaos
The Good, The Bad and The Dad
The Trouble with Order

Short story collections
This Unusual Life!
Some Things That Don't Make Sense

Excerpt from Santa's Sacking

Small town M/X Christmas romance published under my pen name Jaxon Knight

D ec 16th

HR sent a message twenty minutes before it was due to happen.

That was it, no warning, no build up, no time to bolster themself, just a mere twenty minutes was all Darian was given even after working at BirdTalk for most of their career as a software developer.

No respect at all.

Darian sighed and turned to Cathy, their most trusted tester. "It was nice working with you."

Just a month ago, they might have said that on their way to an innocent one-on-one with their bosses, and the two of them would have both known it was a joke. Cathy would have laughed.

It was an old joke, one they would make all the time. But now?

Now Cathy looked haunted; bags under her eyes like she hadn't slept in a week, nails bitten to the quick and a sheen to her skin.

Not haunted, Darian corrected themself. Hunted.

She looked hunted.

Darian imagined they looked much the same. They had been avoiding mirrors since the BirdTalk sale.

The new CEO who was a known edgelord and right-wing tyrant. Nole Ox, a self-professed "self-made genius" who in reality, was the first son of a family rich in blood diamond trade from the last hundred years. The company, everyone knew, was going down the toilet, the question had simply been 'when?'

Darian picked up a battered old notebook they used for problem solving and remembering actions from meetings and made their way down the hall to the meeting room they'd used a thousand times before. Well aware that this time would be their last.

Dec 20th

Darian exited the Greyhound at the bus station (really just an old wooden shelter and a sign) at Snowfall, Colorado. Their Birdtalk branded laptop bag slouched off their shoulders and in their hand they carried a large tote bag of gifts that needed wrapping, the novel they'd been reading resting on top.

Darian shivered. How had they forgotten how *cold* it got in Snowfall?

They should have known. They grew up here, and it was December. No snow had settled on the ground yet, but soon there'd be a big fall and the drifts would be everywhere. The light lambswool sweater that had gotten them through SoCal winters just fine wasn't up to this job.

Darian looked around for their parents.

They shivered again, nervous this time. The town looked so similar, just how they remembered it, with a line of shops on Main St, Minnie's bar at the end of it where Darian earned their first hangover. The massive ski emporium just visible behind it that was super busy in the ski season but they had no idea how it stayed open the rest of the year.

What if Darian's parents hadn't come?

Maybe they thought it was the next bus? Or something had happened, an accident maybe, or emergency?

Darian collected their suitcase from the side of the bus and looked around, trying not to panic. A taxi pulled out over the road and behind it were their parents, heading towards them. Bella and Don, looking just how they always did, but older. More weathered. It had been months since Darian had seen them in the flesh. Damn - they should visit more.

Bella's face crumpled into a sad, sympathetic smile as Darian wheeled their imported, hard case, all-direction-wheeled suitcase towards them.

"Look at you!" Bella wrapped her arms around Darian and hugged them tight. "Horrible business. You're better off out of it. It's been all over the news, that awful man."

"I bet it has," Darian said. Bella smelled of vanilla and cinnamon. "Have you been baking?"

"Yes."

Darian smiled, comforted. Bella's baking was the best in the world. They could practically already taste the sugar cookies and gingerbread.

"Now, your old room is all ready for you, fresh sheets and everything." Bella let go of Darian and half pushed them into Don's arms. He hugged Darian even tighter, if that was possible.

"We've even got a little project lined up for you, to take your mind off things," Don said.

A chill went down Darian's neck that had nothing to do with the winter weather.

"Ma, Dad, I don't need a project."

"Of course you do," Bella said.

"I was just gonna rest for a bit, decompress, reassess, you know? Take stock. Make a plan." Hhow many planning meeting buzzwords could they fit into a single speech? "Plus, I need to wrap my Christmas presents."

"You can do that while you help out," Bella said. "We already signed you up, so you're going to have to do it."

Darian was ushered to the six-month-old electric SUV that they'd bought their parents when they were still earning big Birdtalk dollars, still futilely arguing their case.

Dec 21st

"The Christmas market is featuring a nativity play this year, with the kids from the elementary school starring. They've been practicing for weeks, and I think you'll be very surprised at how eloquent they are." Bella wouldn't let them get a word in. Maybe to deter Darian from explaining once more why they couldn't help out with the Christmas market/Nativity play?

Darian had hoped to spend this, their first day in their extended holiday visit, in bed, sleeping and feeling sorry for themself, but Bella had insisted they get up at 8:00 am, have a hearty breakfast of eggs and toast and accompany her down to the site of the market.

The town hall opened out to a wooded path that led to a gazebo. The market usually took place down the path, with some stalls inside, and hot mulled cider being served from the gazebo. Bella parked right outside the hall itself.

"I have to get to school, but I'll leave you the car. Go in, meet Gary and Vanessa, and see what you're needed for. Have a nice day, sweetie, and I'll see you back home. Your father will pick me up from school."

Bella tossed Darian the keys, grabbed her bag from the back of the car and was gone, hurrying up the road in her snow boots. Darian sat in the passenger seat and stared at the town hall. They contemplated just sliding over, driving back to their parent's house, and getting back into bed. But then Bella would just do the same thing the next day and be all *disappointed* about it.

Also with the way news spread in Snowfall the whole town would know if they didn't show up. Darian would be branded a no-good do-nothing who refused to help out at Christmas. It would probably be in the Snowfall community newspaper.

Far better to go in, explain that they had no skills beyond software and app development and foosball, and let them down easy.

They locked up the car and went inside. "Hello? Uh, my mother sent me?" Darian cringed at how incredibly weak that sounded.

"Back here!" The voice was warm, enthusiastic, and very like Bella's. Darian headed towards it. "You must be Darian!"

"I guess I must." Darian mumbled.

A bright faced woman in a fleece vest over a floral blouse appeared from behind a giant Christmas tree. She had a trim black bob with stripes of gray through it. "I'm Mindy Park, I'm organizing the Christmas festival this year." She shuffled her clipboard under one arm and held her hand out to Darian.

"I thought it was a market, not a festival," Darian said. They took her hand and shook it, she had a firm, no-nonsense grip.

"We're rebranding," Mindy said. "The word festival evoked parties, fun, and community. Market well, market just says 'buy things'."

"I suppose it does."

"Now, we need you to program the lights and the music for the pageant. Of course, you can just do it live with the mixing board, but your mother said you were a genius coder, so I'm sure it will be easy for you to automate it all."

Darian's eyebrows shot up. "Oh, but, I have no experience at all with sound mixing or stage lights."

Mindy flapped her hand and commenced fussing. "You'll pick it up in no time. Smart kid like you. I've seen what happened with BirdTalk on the news, just awful. You're better off back here, reconnect with your roots. Relax. That big city life is toxic after all." She had started ushering Darian towards a booth to the left of the stage.

Darian felt once again that the wall of chat was to stop them arguing. She'd called them a kid and they were twenty-six years old. But that was three topics ago. They sighed, looked at the booth filled with unfamiliar machinery and wires and thanked the stars that they had wifi out in Snowfall, and they could Google this stuff. They noted, briefly, that the wifi was strong, and fast. That certainly hadn't been the case the last time they were in Snowfall.

Mindy showed them the basics that she knew, pointed out the operation manual, game Darian a list of the tracks that the school had requested to be played, and left them to it.

The school. Darian assumed it was their own mother who had sent over this list, since she was so deeply involved in the production. They shrugged off their coat (brown, wool, borrowed from Dad) and tentatively opened the paper manual.

"Mindy!" The most beautiful man they'd ever seen strolled in from the wings of the stage with a toolbox in one hand. He had trim brown hair and an artful amount of scruff on his jaw, broad shoulders and a chest that made Darian's mouth water. His eyes were bright, brown with flecks of something more golden, and he wore a plaid shirt over beat up jeans and boots. Darian was reminded forcefully of their teen crush on Luke from Gilmore Girls.

"Mindy!" the man, the lumberjack angel, repeated.

Darian waved a hand tentatively. "I think she went out somewhere?" They mentally rolled their eyes at themself. Way to state the obvious and make a brilliant first impression.

The beautiful, rugged, man's gaze swiveled to take in Damian. His expression of annoyance softened ever so slightly.

"Oh, hey there. You must be Bella's kid."

Kid. The second time in ten minutes. Darian rankled.

"I'm Darian, I'm twenty six, and up until very recently I was earning six figures at the leading social media company in Silicon Valley." They sounded prim, snobby, and annoying, but they couldn't help it. Perhaps it was the pressure of the last few days. Or the desperate need to do absolutely nothing which had been denied them.

It had all welled up inside and exploded out in a manner Darian despised even as they couldn't stop themself.

The man's eyebrows raised significantly and he held up his hands in a 'hold fire' gesture. "Right, sorry. I didn't mean to offend you, I just... you look younger than twenty six."

Darian deflated entirely. "Yeah, I get that a lot. Sorry, I didn't mean to snap, I'm just..." They scrubbed the back of their sleeve over their eyes. "Just really tired." They felt dangerously close to crying all of a sudden, which was both more childlike and absolutely humiliating. They were *not* crying in front of the hottie. Especially since they'd snapped at him. They swallowed the urge down and blinked up at him. "I mean, I'm sorry."

The man moved closer. "Hey. You want to take a break? There's a really good coffee place a block away."

"I just got here." Darian mumbled into their sleeve. Then they took stock of themself: tired out, emotional for no real reason, overwhelmed with being asked to take charge of something they knew nothing about. They dropped their hand, looking up at the stranger with what they hoped wasn't complete desperation. Just a little desperation would be fine. "But yeah. That sounds great."

"My name's Connor," the man said. "Come on, if we're quick they might not have sold out of apple cinnamon muffins."

Want to read more? Santa's Sacking is available on all good book platforms and in paperback <3